This is the story of a happy year spent by two young Jamaican brothers on their grandfather's small farm, and of a particular event that made the year memorable.

A remarkable re-creation of life in the Jamaican countryside before the days of electricity, THE CLOUD WITH THE SILVER LINING rings with the gaiety of the people and is filled with the warmth of the Jamaican sun.

THE CLOUD
WITH THE SILVER LINING

THE CLOUD
WITH THE SILVER LINING

by C. Everard Palmer

Illustrated by Laszlo Acs

Pantheon Books

c.4

Contents

THE CLOUD
WITH THE SILVER LINING

··{1}··
Runaway!

In those days Boswell was the cream of villages to me. Not that it isn't now and perhaps even more so, with its paved roads and a new school and the many beautiful houses that have sprouted up erect and solid out of concrete and lit with electricity passing on poles. But with all these it has lost something.

Then, the woodlands were near at hand and they were full of birds and each boy carried a slingshot as a matter of course. Vines of all sizes and kinds hung from the treetops like tails, and we boys scrambled into the trees and cut them for skipping-ropes. Skipping was for boys and girls alike.

The river tumbled out of the hill country to our village, snug in the broad valley. Here it sauntered about in loops, curving lazily as if it didn't have a mind to leave our Boswell. The bamboo trees sprouted from the riverbanks and there were reeds where the river idled, tall reeds that harbored frogs galore. But the best things about the river were the pools it provided for bathing and the crayfish it gave up to many a Boswell pot.

We lived in one-, two-, and three-room houses, and our kitchens were always separate shacks walled with wattle-and-daub and roofed with thatch. They were dirt-floored. We lived close, and whoever lit a kitchen fire first in the morning would supply the spark to a good many kitchen fires in his immediate neighborhood. His nearest neighbor would pop through the hedge or over the fence for a light, and another would be supplied by the second, and so it would go on.

The houses, as I have said, were close together. They were small buildings, too, the largest being the Great House of Mister Chaney, the proprietor of the vast banana and sugar-cane estate. The better houses boasted shingle for roofs and zinc sheets too, while others were thatched with the dry heads of the sugar cane bunched together and tied closely to the rafters. Grandpa's house was one of the zinc-roofed ones.

Boswell was not without a square, though a small one, with three shops grouped around it. There was a Baptist church, and also an Anglican church a mile and a half out. And, of course, Boswell had its school.

We boys weren't very stuck on the days from Monday through to Friday noon, because they meant going to school, and school was too serious a place for us. But what weekends we had! They began on Friday afternoon. Saturday was market day at James Bay and, if you were lucky and also re-sourceful and had parents who went to market, you could always earn some quick money. There was always something on the family plot of land to take to market and sell. Milton and I sold our produce, sometimes yams grown in our own fields, sometimes coconuts, mangos if it was the season for mangos, and ginger. Most boys always had ginger to sell.

I particularly liked it when Grandma was alive, because it was she who went to the market each Saturday and, being a woman, she had always needed a boy to handle the donkey for her. If not Milton, then me. But after she died and Grandpa took over, he had no such need for a handler, because he was wise in the ways of donkeys and patient as a crow.

He was actually returning from market on a Saturday afternoon when he met with his terrible accident.

At that time there were three of us living in our house— Grandpa; Milton, my thirteen-year-old brother; and I. Grandpa had a good plot of land, maybe four, maybe five acres in extent. It was partly cultivated with yams, potatoes, bananas, and other crops; and of course there were fruit trees such as mango, breadfruit, and coconut. The part of the land that went uncultivated was occupied by a heifer, which Milton had chosen to call Red Gal, a donkey bought by Grandpa with the name Mirrie, her colt, which Milton and I jointly named Pal Joe, and a goat and kid belonging to Milton. There was a dog, too, Champion by name and very bad-tempered.

There were a few fowl around the house which were mine. When they laid their eggs, they were mine to do whatever I wanted with them, though Grandpa would have frowned upon the idea of my eating them all.

So Grandpa had been returning from the market when he met his accident. He had used the donkey, Mirrie, to take to market the week's produce and the baskets he fashioned. (He made baskets and also fishpots out of bamboo.) They went into hampers (also made by Grandpa) strapped to the animal's back. But Pal Joe was Mirrie's first foal and this particular market outing was her debut since she had borne the little burro. She had never before been forcibly separated from him for a whole day. Being a mother, Mirrie was anxious to be home with Pal Joe and so, said Grandpa when we went to see him in the hospital, she broke into a run the moment he headed her home from James Bay.

Of course, on returning home from market day with a donkey, the handler didn't follow behind. Not at all. The hampers were empty then, anyway, so Grandpa, like anybody else, had climbed atop his mount. He was not too old to restrain Mirrie, though the donkey gave him a stiff fight; but the headrope snapped in the tug-of-war between man and ass, and away she went along the road, galloping full tilt.

Grandpa said he held on, but with a free head Mirrie now galloped wildly. Along the road by the sea, past Lookout Point—the village adjoining James Bay—on to Johnson Corner. Mirrie seemed tireless, the way she kept her pace. In the square at Johnson Corner there was a small knot of men.

"Stop 'er!" Grandpa bawled. "Hold 'er!"

And the men, with flailing arms and shouting voices, had indeed tried to block Mirrie's route. But what are barriers of human bodies to an excited and determined donkey? Mirrie went through them as if they were reeds. They scattered in time, and so the mad gallop home continued. But neither ass nor man arrived.

Mirrie had started to use the road dangerously. She was cutting corners. She got around the first corner safely, and was lucky in negotiating the second: but the third proved her undoing. The corner was a blind one, and though Grandpa heard the truck coming, there was scarcely anything he could have done. Jump off? He would have done so, but he was too slow in making up his mind. Mirrie collided with the truck and she and Grandpa went down in a heap. The money Grandpa had made in the market went flying in all directions, but this was the least of the disaster. Mirrie was so badly hurt that the police from James Bay came and shot her. And Grandpa's right leg was crushed in the accident. He spent four long months in the hospital, where the leg was amputated at the knee.

During his absence, Milton and I were alone at home, try-ing to run things. There was, of course, Allan Bent, our next-door neighbor, who helped us in the fields with the crops and with what animals we had left; and there was his wife, Ethel, who kept an eye on what we were cooking. Grandpa had always paid her to wash our clothes, but now she was doing it free.

We did pretty well in running things. We managed to sell surplus food at home in Boswell, since there was always a grocer willing to buy a bunch of bananas, or the postmistress needing a half-dozen eggs. Everything went almost as when Grandpa was at home, except for the fact that Red Gal broke her tether once or twice and damaged neighbors' crops, and our yard grew up into a near-wilderness from sheer neglect; but then we were so worried about Grandpa.

The car that brought him home from the hospital stopped at our gate, where Allan Bent and Paul Kentish were on hand. They helped him out of the vehicle, but when they attempted to carry him all the way up the hill to the house he protested gruffly.

"Not a bit o' that," he said. "I'm not dead yet."

"But you'll be a long time usin' those crutches up the hill, Mista Cassidy," Allan pointed out.

"No matter," Grandpa said. "I'll be doggoned if I'll allow anybody to lift me up like I was a dratted baby. I can walk. Thanks, gen'elmen," he said. "Thanks a lot."

And he began to swing up the hill on his crutches.

His leg had been amputated at the knee and he had also lost much weight; his muscles sagged. His beard was still at flowing length, but his eyes were dull and sad.

"Hello, boys," he grunted at us when he reached the veranda. He had seen us all the while but he greeted us only after he had sat down in the armchair. He made to lean the crutches against the wall, but Milton stepped forward and took them and did it for him. While he loaded his pipe, he looked at the village sprawling in front of him, looking perhaps for familiar sights.

"How are you, Grandpa?" I asked.

"So-so, boy," he said.

Allan Bent and Paul Kentish asked him the questions that a person returning from the hospital should be asked, then they were ready to depart. They wished Grandpa the very best.

"Thanks a lot, gen'elmen," Grandpa told them. "Thanks for everything."

"You're always welcome, Mista Cassidy," Paul Kentish said.

"It was no trouble at all," said Allan Bent.

They left him then, Allan popping through the hedge to his house across from ours and Paul Kentish heading down the hill to his house. Then, while Milton cooked Grandpa a soup, all those people who had heard of his return came to pay him their respects: Ethel, Allan's wife; Elgin Symes and his wife; Desmond McIntosh; and a couple of others. Grandpa did not talk much but he smoked a lot. When everybody was gone he drank his soup, but he did not talk much with us either, apart from firing a series of questions at Milton.

"How's Red Gal?"

"Fat," Milton said. "Fat, fat, Grandpa."

"Fat, eh?" Grandpa said. "And the foal o' that cussed Mirrie?"

"He's all right, Grandpa. Pal Joe has grown big. You'd be surprised."

"He misses Mirrie a lot," I chirped. "He fretted himself thin, but he's beginning to look good again."

Then he saw the state the yard was in. "Good Lord, son!" he said to Milton. "Why is the yard like this?"

No answer. We looked at it as if we were seeing it for the first time.

"Like a wilderness."

"I'll cut it tomorrow, Grandpa," Milton promised.

"A body'd think I was dead," he said, and puffed away at his pipe, looking round him maybe for something new to criticize. But the floor had been recently scrubbed and polished, and there was no fault he could find with it.

There was still a faint smell of hospital wards on him and, shortly before bedtime, he knocked out a couple of button-sized pills from a vial and swallowed them with a glass of water.

That night in bed Milton whispered to me, "He's worried sick."

"What about?" I asked.

"The loss of his leg, naturally. Who likes to lose a leg and hop around on crutches?"

After a while I asked, "Do you think it will kill him?"

"No. Not if he doesn't fret himself to death. But I think it hurts him that he isn't the same as before."

"Yes," I said.

"He had never been sick, you know, and he was strong and hardy—and now this."

"Yes," I said.

That night I lay awake for a long spell and Milton was also awake. I heard Grandpa turning, too, sleepless as us and maybe more, and one or two times he sighed.

Before a week was out Grandpa had bad news for us. Not so much for me as for Milton.

"We got to sell the cow," he told Milton.

"Red Gal?"

"Yes," Grandpa said. "Which other?"

"But what for, Grandpa?" Milton asked. "Why would we want to sell her?"

"We can't keep her no longer, son. That's why."

"Sure we can. Can't we, Timmy?"

"Yes," I said with power.

Milton sat down at Grandpa's feet and put on his best pleading countenance.

"It needs a man to keep a cow," Grandpa said, and puffed smoke as if he were a steam train.

"But . . ."

"I'm no longer in business."

"But there's me and there's Allan Bent."

"And it costs money to keep a cow too, son."

"Not so much, Grandpa," Milt pleaded.

"Money for rope," Grandpa went on, heedless.

We didn't have a pasture we could let Red Gal loose in, so she was always tethered by a rope in the vacant part of Grandpa's plot.

"But we buy rope only about four times a year, Grandpa," Milt said. He turned to me. "Isn't that so, Timmy?"

I made my answer a very definite yes.

But Grandpa wasn't joking. He let loose with a lot of talk.

"Son," he said, "listen to me. It's got so I can't move round no more. I can't go to the field as I used to, an' there's no one round here who's able to look after that cow properly."

"But I—"

"Shh. You're not big enough nor experienced enough to be responsible for a cow. She busted that rope twice when I was in the hospital, didn't she? An' she'll do it again. What'll happen then, when she goes gallivantin' all over the place, son? She'll go eatin' Allan's banana suckers, make hash o' John Brown's cane sprouts an' Tom Stroke's yams. Destroy this man's field, trample another's rice . . . You know, don't you? An' who'll pay then? Where'll the money be comin' from? I got none left . . ." He was gesticulating. "That cow got to go. I can't see it no other way. Drat!"

I didn't know what to think, but Milton, it seemed, knew, because he was fighting back.

"Listen, Grandpa," he was saying, "there's nothing to it. While you were in the hospital I took good care of Red Gal, didn't I? Saw to it she was put into a fresh patch of grass each day, didn't I? And watered her each evening, didn't I?"

"Ah, that's nothin'. There's nothin' to that."

"And I had Allan Bent keep an eye on things, too, Grandpa."

"Son, we can't depend on others day after day like that. Moreover, the time is comin' when we won't be able to afford a rope. What then? Eh? What then?" He was smoking and snorting. "You go to Johnson Corner and tell Riggan I got a cow I want to get off my hands."

Riggan was the butcher. He slaughtered beef cattle for the local market, pigs and goats as well.

Milton was almost in tears when he heard Grandpa. Red Gal had come to us in this way: she was the calf of a veteran milker owned by Mister Chaney, but shortly after her birth her mother died. Mister Chaney's herdsman had found it a nuisance to look after the orphaned calf, and Mister Chaney had sold her dirt cheap to Grandpa. So the calf had come to us weak and unnamed, and Milton had fallen in love with her from the very start and had named her Red Gal by reason of her bright maroon color.

He had nursed the young calf to strength, and I had seen him spend more mornings and afternoons than I can re-member bottle-feeding Red Gal until she was old enough to eat grass. So there was this close bond between Milton and Red Gal and, now that she had to go, my brother was in a pitiful way.

On Wednesday morning Riggan came to look the cow over and bargain for her. He drove up in his mule cart, and I guessed it was his intention to take Red Gal away in the cart if he and Grandpa reached a settlement on the price. Milton was dispatched to the fields to bring in the cow, and I through the hedge to let Allan Bent know that Riggan was there. Allan was to help Grandpa in pricing the animal and pressing for that price.

Allan Bent joined Grandpa and Riggan on the veranda. Then I saw Milton approaching with Red Gal behind him on a rope.

She was fat almost like two cows together, and shiny where the sun struck her. Her maroon coat was very bright. She followed obediently behind Milton and she swished her tail at the flies that were provoking her. She was chewing her cud contentedly, oblivious of the fate that awaited her.

Milton's face was very dark and cloudy, and it was hard to imagine a sadder boy than he.

When Riggan saw Red Gal, he furrowed his brows and he asked, "That the cow?"

"The very one," Grandpa answered.

"Burstin' with fat," Allan Bent commented, as if he meant to settle for a good price at once because of that.

"Bursting with fat my granny!" Riggan almost shouted. "Can't you see the cow's in calf?"

Grandpa's eyes popped.

"In calf?" he gasped. "Impossible!"

"Yes, Mister Cassidy," Riggan said. "Just that. Wait a minute."

He walked down the steps of the veranda and into the yard around Red Gal, seemingly taking an inventory of her.

"She's about six months in calf," he confirmed.

"What the . . . ?" was all Grandpa managed to say. "But how come?" Grandpa was truly baffled.

"I don't know how come," Riggan said professionally, "but she'll be presenting you with a calf mighty soon. That's all I know."

"Well," Allan Bent said, coming up with a theory, "the cow's broken loose a couple o' times an' it must have been one o' these times she broke loose an' wandered. Mister Chaney's got a bull an' Gary Brother's got one up at Junction . . ." Junction was a district two miles to the north of us. "Maybe that's how she got that calf," Allan said.

"I'll be doggoned," Grandpa said, and his jaws were working.

In Milton's face something like fire was burning, because this meant that Red Gal could not be sold now for slaughter.

Riggan was examining Red Gal again. He stooped down and looked at the udder which, to me, had not changed one bit in size. "She's in calf, sure. She'll perhaps be having calf in . . . now is October . . ." he paused to think and to calculate, ". . . I wouldn't be surprised if she drops that calf in early December."

"You don't say!" Allan Bent said.

"Sure I mean it," Riggan said. "Any blind man can see she's in calf."

"Well, to be frank, I didn't get much of a chance to see the animal these last weeks," Allan said. "I passed 'er only at a distance, an' I never took much of a close look at 'er."

I guessed he was trying, with this excuse, to make himself look less an amateur with cows.

"Well, I'll be doggoned," Grandpa said. "In calf! What'll I do now?"

"Why sure, keep her," Riggan encouraged him. "Keep her, Mister Cassidy. Only a few weeks more and she'll have her calf and you'll be having milk."

"Take 'er away, Milton," Grandpa said, annoyed. "Take that dratted cow away."

The morning sun glinted on Milton's teeth. He was smiling as he turned away. Keep her. A calf in December and then milk. Sale for the milk. Money. Enough to buy rope to hold Red Gal secure, and something over, too, to feed us and buy some clothes.

"I've got to be going," the butcher announced, business-like. "No sense in my hanging around. There's nothing here for me."

"Thanks for comin', anyway," Grandpa said, completely beaten.

"And thanks too, Mister Riggan," Milton chirped as he led Red Gal away. "Thanks a lot." He raised a hand to Riggan. He was on the verge of happy laughter but you bet he was suppressing it to spare Grandpa more annoyance.

"Okay, Milton," Riggan said. "If the calf turns out to be a bull, I'll butcher him one o' these days."

"That'll be fine with me," Milton assured him.

Riggan stalked down to his cart on the road, and in a moment he was on his way, the cartwheels crunching the stones noisily.

"What'll I do now, Allan?" Grandpa asked.

"Keep 'er as the butcher said. That's the logical thing. The cow'll soon be payin' for 'er keep."

"I don't know. I don't know really," said Grandpa with his chin on his chest and his horny hands locked together on his belly. "I don't know really."

Thereupon Milton led Red Gal to green pastures and everybody was happy except Grandpa.

·{2}··
The Sadness of Big Squeak

Sunday had come and Grandpa was still deep in melancholy. He spoke hardly at all and his chin was always on his chest when he wasn't smoking, which was often.

We were sitting in the kitchen, Milton and I. Grandpa was in the dining room, supposedly having his breakfast. We had just finished ours, which we hadn't bothered to eat inside the house. For us the kitchen was as good a place as the hall-and-dining place.

"Grandpa is very grumpy," Milton began.

"Grumpy?"

"Yes, he's sad and he's hard to please."

"He doesn't talk much," I said.

"Why do you think he wanted to sell Red Gal?"

"Maybe he doesn't like her, Milt."

"No," Milt said. "Not that. I have a suspicion that he's so worried about having to sit around with one leg that maybe he was thinking of using the money from the sale to find a way out."

"What way?"

"Maybe buying a mule and a saddle to ride about."

"Oh," I said. "But that'd be a lot of money, buying a mule and a saddle."

"Yes. But perhaps he thought of doing it just the same. He has missed church a lot. He wants to go to church and he can't because he won't be able to walk the distance."

"And what about the crutches?" I asked.

"He can't use them that far! The church is a good way out from here. A mile and a half. You didn't think he could walk that far on crutches, did you?"

"No," I said. "I didn't think so. Well, the Baptist church is near. Just down the road. Why doesn't he go to the Baptist church for a change?"

"He! You must be crazy. You know Grandpa well enough. He was born an Anglican. He grew up as an Anglican. And you bet he's aiming to die an Anglican."

I wouldn't dispute that. But I wondered about his stubborn wish to go to church.

"I can't understand it," I said. "Why should anyone wish to go to church so badly as to fret about it? Why, if he can't make it—why doesn't he rest content? Me—I wouldn't bother myself if I couldn't go to church! Why, if I had an excuse I wouldn't go to Sunday School this very Sunday to face Miss Kirby! I haven't learned the Scripture verses she asked us to prepare for today. I'd rather stay home. I'd be happy to stay home today."

"That's you, Timmy. And I feel that way sometimes, too. But with Grandpa, it's different. He's been going to church for so many years. Years upon years. He's held two offices.

He was the official bell-ringer until the accident. He loved that job. It made him feel useful. And there was this other job of passing the collection plate around for the offering, too. You've seen him walking up the aisle, holding the plate out."

"*If* I have!" I said. "Sure I have."

"Well, he likes these two jobs. And he likes to stand at the back and roll out his lusty bass. Now he's tied down at home and it's driving him crazy."

I knew what Milton was getting at. In truth Grandpa had always liked these jobs at church, and to take communion there. He walked back and forth in the aisle almost as if he owned the place, and his boots were always squeaking. Why, if Grandpa's boots were not the squeaking type, he would never have worn them out of the house! I didn't know in what way the squeaking appealed to him, but he was mad over boots that squeaked. People nicknamed him Big Squeak, and probably would have called Milton Little Squeak and me Mini Squeak, because Grandpa bought squeaking shoes for us too, but we had gone to work on them, walking in puddles and dew-wet grass and using vaseline to moisten up the leather.

Milton was right about Grandpa. The amputation of his leg, which prevented him from going to church to ring the bell and to pass the collection plate around and to take communion, was killing him. Now Jabesh Gilligan, another old man, with eyes that bulged and a mustache as thick as a hedge, took Grandpa's church roles.

"You watch," Milton said, "when it's time for us to go to church, how much sadder Grandpa will become. He'll think he, too, should be off to church. He'll be thinking of old Jabesh Gilligan ringing the bell and passing around the plate, jobs he ought to be doing. And he'll be a lot sadder."

"Poor Grandpa," I said. "It's awful that he should suffer so."

"Yes," Milt said.

We couldn't have said much more on the subject then, because the first peal of the Boswell Anglican church bell rolled up the valley to us, and that meant time to prepare for Sunday school.

Now, as I came out of the kitchen and passed by Grandpa where he was sitting on the veranda, I watched him for signs of agony and I saw plenty. While the bell-ringing lasted he sat bolt upright, his beardy face in the direction of the church and his eyes narrowed. In the hall I paused and watched and, as the ringing ended, his tense body went flabby and his alertness withered. The life that had only a little while ago throbbed in his face, shrank into his beard and was gone, and his neck lost its strength too, for his head sank slowly to his breast and it was as if he were asleep.

"See what I mean?" Milt said when I joined him in our bedroom. He was already changing into his Sunday best.

"Yes, you're right, Milt," I said.

"Of course I'm right."

"I've never seen a body suffer so as when the bell rang and he was thinking that he should have been the one ringing it."

"We'll have to do something."

"Such as?" I asked.

"I don't know as yet," Milt said, pulling on his shirt.

"Sell Red Gal to a farmer maybe, so that . . ."

Milton didn't give me a chance to get further.

"No," he said, "No!" And he was snorting like a bull.

We were soon dressed in our Sunday best, in suits of white

drill—jacket and shorts—and black socks and shoes. My socks had started to give me trouble, and we had not even begun the long walk to the church. They were slipping from my calves and this was a weekly nuisance, as I wasn't the one who boasted the sort of calves that keep socks up. We wore caps, too, against the hot sun, which always seemed hotter on Sundays.

When we stepped out on to the veranda, Grandpa raised his chin from his breast, but not with any intention of inspecting us for well-brushed hair and teeth, straight neckties, clean fingernails, and polished shoes. He merely looked to see that it was us, and he stretched his hand out with a penny.

"That's all," he said in his throat.

Milton beat me to it and took the offering from Grandpa's horny hand. I began to scowl and to grumble, saying, "Give it to me. I want to carry it."

Grandpa stamped his sound foot hard and growled, "Young man!" and I forgot the grumbling and contrived to look happy beneath his glare.

" 'Bye, Grandpa," Milton said.

"Behave yourselves," Grandpa said.

" 'Bye, Grandpa," I told him.

"And you, young man," he said to me, "don't you let me get a single report about you."

"No, Grandpa."

"Milton, you keep an eye on him."

"I will, Grandpa," Milt said.

So we left the veranda and walked down to the road, and only on occasions as this, going to church, did I ever walk and not bound in leaps down that track. But now, wearing shoes which were tight on my feet, I dared not leap or run and risk scraping my heels or murdering my toes. I took my time down that dirt track, with Milton ahead of me, walking confidently. He was clutching the Bible and I the Prayer Book from which we'd sing once the big service got under way.

I should confess I didn't sing well from this book on account of the hymns being in small print. Each Sunday, while Milton sang away, I'd hold on to one side of the Prayer and Hymn Book and make believe I was really singing, by opening my mouth and attempting to shape the words with my lips.

Now we were on the road and we looked back and saw

Grandpa sitting in the same place and his head was on his breast again, and I guessed he was thinking of yet another service he would be missing. Poor old man, I thought, he'd have liked to be walking along with us instead of sitting back there.

That was how it had always been before the accident. We would breakfast early and tidy up and be at the church by nine o'clock because that was the hour Grandpa rang the first bell.

I can't say that I liked those times better, because the rush to church always interfered with and spoiled a good Sunday breakfast of roasted breadfruit eaten with avocado-pear pegs and with codfish imported from Newfoundland, and with boiled ackee, Jamaica's national fruit. Then there was a mug of steaming hot chocolate for each of us.

Ordinarily we hurried through breakfast and were at the church at nine. Then we had an extra hour to study what Scripture passages Miss Kirby had assigned us, if we hadn't studied them as yet—and usually I hadn't. For let it be understood that although we had a whole hour, which some other boys might have spent playing or searching for lizards, we dared not have done any such thing in our Sunday suits. Not with Grandpa around. No, we would crawl into a pew meekly as doves and study our verses while Grandpa, sitting somewhere behind us and peering over his spectacles dropped low on his nose, read his Bible. He read aloud because Grandpa wasn't the one who thought that reading was reading if it wasn't done aloud.

Now, as I plodded on heavily churchward beside Milton, I looked back and noticed that Grandpa was out of sight, and I remembered the penny that he had given to Milton as offering. Why should *he* have the pleasure of plunking it into the collection plate and not me? Yes, why? So I began to scowl anew and to sniff.

"What's the matter?" he asked. "Your shoes?"

"No," I said and walked briskly, to the detriment of my heels and toes, in my demonstration to him that no shoes could ever make me sniff.

"What then?"

"The penny," I said.

"What about it?"

"You have it," I said.

"Sure I have it. Grandpa gave it to me to drop in the collection plate."

"I want it," was all I said.

"Don't be stupid, Timmy," Milton said. "It's offering money. I'm not going to keep it or spend it!"

"I want it," I said.

"But . . ."

"I want to drop it in," I said.

"Oh, that!"

"Yes," I said. "I want to drop it in."

"Stupid," he said. "You stupid, childish crybaby!"

"Give it to me," I said.

I discerned already that he wasn't particular about having the joy of plunking it into the plate and I knew he would give it to me. With a little pressure. A little more honest-to-goodness sniffing. And I was right, too. His hand went into his pocket and came up with the copper coin, and mine sailed out to his and took the penny.

"There," he said. "And stop making a fool of yourself."

I slipped the coin into my trouser pocket and it felt good and cool under my sweating fingers. The fact was, this was the first time we had ever set off to Sunday school with only a penny between us. I had always had my offering and Milton his, and Grandpa his in a small envelope, as all the other adults. In fact Milton and I had always had two offerings—one for Sunday school and the other for the big service that followed after. This sudden poverty of a single penny was caused by Grandpa's accident. There had been no market-going, few sales of anything, and what little money had been raised had been spent to keep us going.

And in all that time, from the accident to now, Milton and I had been so listless that we had made no effort to sell anything for ourselves.

Of course, Milton didn't have to give up the penny. He could, for instance, have forced me to wait until we reached Mrs. Seggie's sweet shop at Johnson Corner, which was down the road a bit, and there he could have had the penny changed for two half-pennies, which would be as good a solution as any. But he hadn't done that: he had handed over the penny to me and I began to think that perhaps he, too, like Grandpa, was losing interest in things. Unlike Grandpa, however, Milton had lost no limb, come to no harm. But I guessed he was thinking of Grandpa's lost happiness.

We went on without talking, though this was not from any ill feelings on either side. The road was white, almost dazzlingly white, under the harsh morning sun and the gravel crunched like popcorn beneath our shoes. At this point the road was straight, flat, and monotonous, and ran between the endless fields of sugar cane, which came up to the banks like hedges; but soon we left the cane behind and were passing through banana land. The road began to climb. Not sharply but in loops, and this put the banana trees against the sun so that from time to time we were afforded a bit of shade.

All along the road here we passed the piles of dry banana leaves used as wadding for stacked fruits and left behind from the last banana day. That is the name given to any day on which large-scale reaping of the fruit is done for export to countries such as England. As I walked along, the scent of the thrash rotting in its pile was in my nostrils. And there were several trees straining with heavy bunches of banana, some ripe and ready for the next banana day; some almost so; others only now appearing thin-fingered from the bulky, scaly, bullet-shaped buds.

The road began to fall away on the other side of the hill and we soon came within earshot of the Boswell River, gurgling as it passed over and between the stones. Abruptly, the road made a deep loop and we were on the Broad Gate bridge. I stopped for a peep over the rails and down into the clear pool that formed as the water left the spillway. Small fish were moving in the water.

Milton was some way ahead when I finally moved off the bridge, and I ran to catch up with him. Of course by now I could afford to run. We had walked more than a quarter of a mile and my feet were no more strangers to the shoes. It was always that way: a quarter of a mile or so of walk and my feet became seasoned to the leather.

A truck came along the road, churning dust, and left us in a cloud. It was good that this was Sunday and, with luck, we wouldn't meet any more before we reached the church.

I learned very little in Sunday school that day. I was hot all through and mischievous too, and maybe more than all bored. Miss Kirby, our teacher, was continually mad at me, pulling off her glasses to roll her eyes at me.

"Timmy, sit down!"

"Timmy, turn around!"

"Boy in the corner, look this way! And leave the other boy's ear alone!"

Finally she took me out of the corner and stuck me under her nose in the front pew. That did it. I gave no more trouble for the day.

At last, however, Sunday school broke up and the church began to fill up with adults, mostly women swinging hand fans to keep themselves cool. I was suffering from the heat inside too, so I took a walk around to where the bell was hanging from the tree. Formerly the bell used to be high in a belfry, but the latter had been destroyed by a storm and so the bell had been hung by a chain from a tree. Grandpa used to ring it properly with a rope, but now old Jabesh Gilligan was holding on to the tongue and slamming it against the bell-circumference. The bell sounded out harsh and loud, but at least it was rhythmic.

Jabesh was at the bell-ringing for more than fifteen minutes and the harshness of the bell had become so irritating that when he finally stopped everyone was relieved. Everybody now settled down inside, waiting for Parson Jackson to arrive. We at the windows all looked out to see his car come chugging up the hill, but our vigil was in vain. Then the word got around that he would be later than usual and that Leon Tanner, a kind of stand-in preacher, would keep things going until the parson arrived.

Leon Tanner indeed!

Leon was a World War I veteran. Whenever he was dressed up—and he was dressed up now—he made no bones about advertising that fact, wearing his medal high on his lapel. It would not be inappropriate to say that he was quite a boaster. He crunched up the aisle now, his legs putteed as a soldier's or a horseman's, and his mustache, twirled at the ends, hung out as wide as his face. Some people claimed you could hang a hat on Leon Tanner's mustache and it would take the load. Like Grandpa's, his boots squeaked. He reached the pulpit and he stood there looking through the great thick Bible, wetting a thumb on his tongue and flipping the pages until he found what he was looking for. Then he tiptoed over to the organist —but with all his tiptoeing his boots squeaked—and he discussed selection of hymns with her.

Back in the pulpit, Leon Tanner puffed out his chest like a prize bird. "The hymn number . . ." and Leon Tanner called out the hymn, punishing the R in "number" with a lengthy roll on his tongue.

The organist, a fat woman, struck out with some notes to acquaint the congregation with the tune of the hymn and the timing; then we all stood, and the next moment everybody was making a joyful noise unto the Lord. At the close of the hymn, Leon held his arms out like a bird sunning itself and, in his best intoning voice, said: "Let us pray." Some of us sat and levered forward, while the more pious, the adults mostly, knelt properly. He was long in praying, and even in reading the Bible he was long too, choosing the longest chapters. But now he was through and he raised his head and opened his eyes.

Everybody sat up. Leon Tanner went on and said a few words of welcome and explained briefly that the rector had been delayed by car trouble. How we boys looked at one another and wished we were somewhere along the road helping Parson Jackson and getting greased up and all! But Leon Tanner went on and summoned up his best pulpit manners and began to read the Bible. He would have gone on with more of the service, had not Parson Jackson arrived.

Parson went through all the rites, which were what I liked

—the standing and the kneeling and the chanting, he intoning one thing and we answering with another. When he was finished, he expressed joy at seeing everyone there and he said a word of welcome to friends and well-wishers.

Then it was communion time. The whole scene became solemn and righteous, and I saw perfectly clearly why Grandpa missed it so.

When the last hymn had been sung, Jabesh Gilligan ambled up the aisle bowlegged as a man who had spent many years in the saddle. He passed the collection plate along the pews on both sides of the aisle. His chest was out and he licked his lips as he performed this service for the Lord. When the plate reached me, I held my penny high and let it plunk down onto the other coins. An old woman looked at me sternly, rolling her eyes, but I had done it already and I was happy.

The moment the service was over, the older people thrashed for the door and lined up there, because shaking hands with the preacher was a part of the service to them.

I had seen enough. Yes, Milton was right. Somehow or other we'd have to think of a way to aid Grandpa in getting back to church. A way, that is, which would exclude the selling of Red Gal. Grandpa would probably not be able to hold down his former jobs, such as ringing the bell and walking the aisle with the collection plate, but he could at least be there to add his bass to the singing and to take the sacrament.

·∙{3}∙·
The Fishpot

Immediately after this, Monday morning to be exact, I noticed that Milton was working toward something. He was, it seemed, straining at restoring order in our house. This, to me, was not a bad thing because order, according to the teachings of Miss Kirby, was Heaven's first rule. Milton soon presented me with a timetable. It was elaborate.

	Rise
	Feeding fowls: Timmy
	Drawing fishpot: Timmy
MONDAY	*Attending Red Gal, Pal Joe, goats: Milton*
TUESDAY	*Breakfast: Milton*
WEDNESDAY	*Dishes: Washing—Milton; drying—Timmy*
THURSDAY	*School*
FRIDAY	*After school: Red Gal, Pal Joe, goats—Milton*
	Dinner: Milton
	Dishes: Washing—Milton; drying—Timmy
	Setting fishpot: Milton and Timmy
	Homework

Rise
Fowls: Timmy
Fishpot: "
Animals: Milton
Breakfast: Milton
Dishes: As Monday through to Friday
SATURDAY *Firewood: Milton and Timmy*
Cleaning up: "   "
Dinner: Milton
Dishes: As above
Fishpot: Milton and Timmy
Grocery: Milton and Timmy
After: Anything goes

Rise
Fowls: Timmy
Fishpot: "
Animals: Milton
Breakfast: "
SUNDAY *Dishes: As above*
Sunday school
Dinner: Milton
Dishes: As above
After: Anything goes

I didn't think that I had gotten everything right the first time, so I went through the schedule slowly once more. Then I spotted a flaw.

"What do you mean I'll draw a fishpot?" I asked. "What pot? There's no fishpot!"

"I know," Milton said.

"So why put that in?"

"Because we'll be having a pot, that's all."

"Oh! How, my man? And when?"

"How? By having Grandpa make us one—that's how. But when I can't say as yet."

"Let's go right now and ask him."

"No," Milton said with the wisdom of an oracle. He pulled

up his brows and half-winked one eye at me. "We'll do it another way, Timmy. We'll get the material to make the pot first, have it right on the spot here in the yard, before we ask Grandpa. Then, when we pop the big request, it won't be easy for him to say no. He'll say to himself. 'Well, they have brought the bamboo already, and it would break their hearts after such work and hoping, if I denied them the pot.' He'll say something like that you bet. What do you think?"

"That's a sound idea," I said. "That's smart, Milt. Real smart."

I liked handling a fishpot. Both the setting of it in a pool and its withdrawal from that pool. Especially when the pot caught fish. We had always had fishpots, but they never usually lasted out a year. One night you'd go to bed and there'd be heavy rain and the river would come flooding and wash away the pots. Of course we made a weather forecast of sorts by reading the clouds before we set the pots, and if the clouds promised rain we canceled setting that evening. But if the sky was clean or had clouds that were white through and through, we set. Even with these precautions taken, however, we lost our pots to the river. There was always the surprise rain in the night.

The other boys had to buy their pots, but Milton and I got ours free. Grandpa was the maker of fishpots, so he made ours for us. The other boys obtained theirs, also manufactured by Grandpa of course, through their parents, who had to pay for them. Of course, if a boy could not persuade his parents to buy him a pot and if he were on friendly terms with either Milton or me, we talked Grandpa into making him a pot free, providing he supplied the bamboo.

Grandpa worked at his craft beneath a spreading guango tree in our yard, and the pile of waste from the bamboo he

stripped down for his fishpot- and basket-craft was visible
from where we were standing now. Only there was no new
waste on the pile, and that was because he had been so long
away at the hospital, during which time his craft had been
shelved. I could only hope that he would indeed slip out of
his melancholy and make us that fishpot.

"Any more questions?" Milton asked, referring to the
timetable.

"Let's see," I said and read on down until I came to Saturday. I read:

> Fowls: Timmy
> Fishpot: "

"How come I'm not drawing the fishpot on a Saturday?"
I asked, a little bit mad.

"Of course you are," Milton said.

"But I see 'Fishpot' and then beside it two strokes," I said.

"That means you," Milt said.

"It's not my name," I said.

"It's a ditto mark and it means 'same as above,'" Milton
said, and laughed at me.

"Oh," I said, feeling ignorant.

"Any more questions?"

"Yes," I said after reading on. "What do you mean, 'Anything goes' on Saturday and Sunday after we are through
with everything?"

"You know," he explained, "the usual thing. We do as we
feel like. Just as before. On Saturday evening we can saunter
down to the square and look around a bit and on Sundays—
well, there isn't much we can do on that evening."

I understood. A Sunday in Boswell, in those days, was almost dangerous for a boy. On this day, any of the usual activi-
ties of boys could bring down the strap from its hook, or a

belt from a waist if that were more handy. Adults didn't take Sunday lightly as they do now. They maintained it was the Sabbath and a holy day and should be given—every minute, ay, every second of it—to the Lord. Nothing resembling a game was tolerated. So a boy innocently throwing a stone could be put over the knee for practicing a ball game on the Sabbath. Or two of them performing an errand and running could be stopped on the road and reminded in the most practical of ways that Sunday was not a day for playing a game of chase. It was like that in Boswell when I was a boy. The only people who got away with a breach of the Sabbath were the shopkeepers. They were not permitted, by law, to sell goods on Sundays, but they obliged customers by opening a window and selling through it. Nobody said much about this because it was maintained the shopkeepers weren't barefaced about it. They were using a window, not the door.

On the contrary, a Saturday evening in Boswell was great fun. We went to the square, and almost everybody else went there at some time or other in the course of the evening. The people shopped then for the coming week, and parents gave children what pocket money they could afford. The children spent what they had been given or realized from selling their own produce, and it was just grand on a Saturday evening. It was in the evening that the district's musicians took out their guitars and banjos and fifes and walked with them to the square. They didn't form into anything like an orchestra, but they played music and, though there wasn't regular street dancing, a body could loosen up his bones if he had a mind to.

"Anything goes," said Milton's timetable! That was all right with me. I had no more questions to ask. No, siree! The timetable was satisfactory.

"No more questions," I said.

"Satisfied?"

"Pleased," I said.

"All right."

Working with Milt in the days that followed took on a different meaning for me. It wasn't just routine as it had been before. It seemed as if I had enlisted my services for a cause.

For the first week Milton let the fishpot scheme alone, but, with me reminding him night and day about it, he finally decided to put our little plan to work.

Grandpa was still a melancholy old soul. He talked very little, and by remaining indoors a great deal, he avoided shouting back a greeting to people who passed on the road. He waited for the night to darken the land and then he'd move out on to the veranda and he'd smoke there. But when Grandpa wasn't smoking, his head was usually on his breast.

We went down to the river to get the bamboo and we took Champion, our dog, along with us. While we selected and toppled a tall, sleek-trunked bamboo tree, Champion roved in the shrubs, his tongue lolling out. When it got too warm for him, he plunged into the river in a nearby pool and swam around in it. We could have used a swim too, but we denied ourselves and picked up our load and tramped back to the house.

Milton was in front and I behind. The stouter part of the trunk rested on his shoulder and the slim section was on mine. There was about sixty feet of bamboo between us. That way we carried back the tall bamboo.

When we threw it down it made a noise, and Grandpa looked out and down the incline to the guango tree and saw it.

"What's it for?" he asked Milton, when we went up to the house.

"A fishpot, Grandpa."

"H'm," he said, sitting again in his armchair. "Didn't think you knew how to make one, son."

"I *don't*, Grandpa. I brought the bamboo for *you* to make it."

"Me?"

"Yes, Grandpa," Milt said with a straight face.

"Look, son . . ."

"But Grandpa," Milton began in his best pleading voice. And that did it.

"Drat it," Grandpa said irritably. "Dratted fishpot. Every year a fishpot, a fishpot. And in the end it's that river that gets it."

"We need the pot, Grandpa."

"Need it or not, if you hadn' 'a' brought that bamboo along already, there wasn't going to be no fishpot. Drat!"

So Milton's wisdom really paid off. I was happy already.

The following day, a Saturday, Grandpa dragged himself out of the house to start work on the pot. Using his crutches he swung across the yard and down to the shade beneath the guango tree. I carried a bench for him to sit on and Milton had, to Grandpa's specifications, whetted a cutlass to perform the task of cutting the bamboo up into strips. The knife that would shave down the strips was honed by Grandpa himself. As he reached the old pile of waste near which he would work, the old man looked around him and sniffed the air, filling his lungs. The air from the river was cool and fresh and it seemed to remind him of the days, now gone, when he had spent most of his waking hours outdoors. Abruptly he set to work, deftly cutting up the bamboo trunk into strips.

The pot was finished that same day. In its completed state a pot has the shape of a top, almost a cone. The funnel-shaped entrance is centered in the broad base, and the exit, to be closed

when it is in the water, is in the tapering end. Its woven walls
let the water seep in whenever it is laid in the river and out
again the moment it is raised.

We decided we would set the pot that very evening at dusk.
It would mean drawing it from the water on Sunday morning,
but this would be considered a necessity and not a violation of
sabbatical code.

With roasted coconut flesh we baited the pot, adding bits
of broken white chinaware, the whiteness in the water to act
as added lure. As ballast we loaded in a couple of stones. A
leash was attached to the pot, this leash to prevent it—barring
floods—from being moved downstream, and also to serve to
lift the pot from the depths.

The first night was like any other first night of pot-setting.
The Saturday evening fun in the square missed us, so anxious
were we over the pot. And the moment we got to the square
we wanted to leave for home again, as if going home meant a
speed-up of the night. Neither Milton nor I slept very well.
We woke several times.

"Sleeping?"

"No."

"Is it time?"

"Let's take a look."

So we opened a window and looked out, but dawn never
seemed near. Each time we looked the moon had moved from
its last position high in the sky, but it was still not anywhere
near dropping out of sight behind the hill. So back to bed we
went to have more catnaps until, after an interminably long
time, dawn erupted with the crowing of cocks and the chirp-
ing of birds. Fowls were flying off their roosts when we
dashed out of the house and down to the river where we had
set the pot.

It should be noted that on that first morning it wasn't Timmy alone, as provided by the timetable, who went to draw the pot. Milton was so anxious to see what success we'd start off with that he was ahead of me in the dash to the pool. It was *he* who drew the pot out of the water, too; not me. Quickly he loosened the leash from the shrub to which we had tied it, and gently he pulled at it. Up came the pot slowly, breaking the surface. The water seeped out fast, and he first, and I after, took a look through the funnel-shaped entrance.

"Nothing," he said, passing the pot to me. "Not even one."

There was indeed no fish in the pot except for a few tiny crayfish that some people called Jumpin' Jones, because of their obsession with jumping. They were tiny and they were worthless. I shook the pot so that the bait—still there except for small nibbles by the Jumpin' Jones—and the ballast shifted. I was hoping that a fish would show up from beneath them. But nothing showed. There was nothing in there.

"Well?" I said.

"There'll be better luck next time," Milt said.

"I think so too," I said.

"We'll certainly catch something the next time out," he declared.

"And why not?" So we consoled each other. Of course the chances of catching any fish the first night out were always slim, because a new fishpot had a smell of its own, just like a new book or a new car, and in the water for the first night it was without the scent of the river. Any wise fish was justly wary of unfamiliar shapes and smells, even if such shapes contained the powerful scent of roasted coconuts.

We trudged back to the house, not very anxious to report such a disappointment to Grandpa. But he had no word of derision for our failure. This was Sunday and, nowadays, the

old man's worst day. Church day. On this day the world could
have ended for all he cared. He was not a part of it.

We did our jobs, had breakfast, prepared for Sunday school,
and left him on the veranda, sitting in the armchair, his head
on his chest, and he didn't ask anything about the fishpot.
Something had to be done about that old man.

On Monday at dusk again Milton and I went back to set
the pot. Milton decided he would set the pot in the same pool.
It was a long pool and oval-shaped, and it had rocks at both
ends and a tree to one side with roots kneeling in the water.
This was an ideal place, declared Milton. He said there were
holes under the rocks and between them where fish lived, and
there had to be fish in the pool. We called this pool Grandé
Hole.

Milton tossed the baited pot in with a motion as of a cow-
boy using a lasso. It landed in the center of the pool with a
crish, not a *crash*, and sent several circles of water racing to
the banks. Then it sank slowly.

The following morning Milton did not accompany me to
draw the pot. He made an excuse about wanting to go look
after Red Gal and Pal Joe and his goats early and be back in
time, but I thought he was scared of another disappointment.
So it was Timmy alone who drew the pot and, even before
I raised it high enough to see, I knew it had fish in it. I heard
the batter of fishtail against the bamboo wicker-work and I
burst out into happy laughter. I turned the pot over and over
in my hands, counting the fish as they appeared.

One, I counted.

Two, I counted.

Three!

The third was a big crayfish with dangerous-looking claws.
It moved ponderously over the ballast in the pot and I guessed

it was heavy. With the pot on my shoulder and water from it dripping on my clothes, I began my run back to the house.

On my way I ran into Josh Tingling, another Boswell boy.

"What you got there, Timmy? Eh?"

Josh knew a fishpot all right, but all the same he asked the unnecessary question.

"Fishpot," I said.

"Caught anything?" he asked.

"Sure."

"What, Timmy? What?"

"Three," I shouted as I breezed on.

"Let's have a look, Timmy," he said, running behind me.

"No time, Josh," I said, still running.

"Not even for a marble?"

That changed the picture. I pulled up, and after he had deposited a handsome marble in my hand, I gave him a brief look in the pot.

"Wow!" he said, his eyes popping. "Look at that one!"

He meant the giant. But I didn't comment. I was on my way again.

At the house I shook Grandpa under the blanket.

"Fish," I said excitedly. "The fishpot caught three."

"Uh," he said, and I remembered that with Grandpa nothing mattered. So I ran along the track to the fields to pass the good news on to Milton. I met him coming home.

"Fine," he said. "Are they big?"

"One is a giant," I said. "The other two are medium-sized."

"Good," he said, and he made no attempt to conceal his happiness.

I showed him my marble and told how Josh Tingling had been glad to pay it for a look at our catch. But that didn't seem to impress him. My keenness in business meant nothing to him.

At home, when the exit of the pot was opened, the fish crawled out and began a jumping spree in the grass, and Champion barked at the sight of them. Milton carefully transferred them to a pan of water in which they would remain alive until cooking time.

In the kitchen I had a question. "What'll we do with them?"

"Eat them."

"I mean, how? In what fashion?"

"We'll make a soup," he said. "We've been eating too much codfish and pork of late."

Which was true.

"We've been short of money, and codfish being cheap we've bought a lot. But it's no good eating so much of it. Grandpa'll like the soup for a change."

"And it'll do him good," I said.

"As the pot continues to work for us we'll save money," Milton said. "With some money saved, after a while, we'll be able to do something for Grandpa."

"Hey!" I said. "That'll take a long time, won't it? There isn't much money to be saved from not buying codfish."

"You are a pessimist," Milton said.

"A pessi-what?"

"I mean you are a quitter. You give up too easily. You lose hope at a word. Remember, big things start small," he said, and he sounded like a great teacher.

"I'm not giving up hope either," I said.

"You must have faith," he said.

The fishpot caught fish steadily for us, and when we didn't make soup with them, we ate them curried and sometimes, too, poached. It soon got around that we were operating with a fishpot, because Josh Tingling, who had seen me with it, had talked. Cal Symes, who lived on the ridge next to ours, also saw it and talked. Several other boys at various other times had seen us with it and they wanted to have pots to set in the river too, but who was there to make them theirs? Not Grandpa, who only said, "Drat it," when inquiries were made of him. "That's the only one I'll be makin' this time."

The other boys had to be content with catching fish on the hook, which was a time-consuming way and not always rewarding, since they fished in the daytime, when crayfish don't move about as much as at nighttime. The boys didn't hold any grudge against us though. They merely considered us lucky, and everything went well until one morning, when I was returning from the river with the pot, I ran into Jester.

Jester was Boswell's boy-bully. He was ropy-muscled and strong and he had never been to school.

"Let's see what you got there," he said.

My heartbeat quickened as he said it. He was some way off to one side of the track and was engaged in target practice with his slingshot. A breadfruit hanging from its branch was the target. As he walked over now to confront me, he began to stuff the slingshot into his pocket, and I had a quick impulse to run for it. So I did just that.

"Hold it!" he said as he sprinted after me, but I didn't even look back. I made tracks and when I turned in at my gate, he still had not caught up with me.

"Come, Champion! After him, Champ!" I called, although I knew very well that our dog was on a chain. But he heard me and roared and barked and Jester, knowing the disposition of Champion, made a discreet stop.

When I stood safe by the veranda, I dropped the pot and looked back. Jester was down in the road threatening me. He made a fist and pointed it in my direction; then he put the

fist in his eyes and rubbed it around, which was a way of saying he would blacken my eye. Then he went away. I told
Milton.

"Oh, he won't do anything."

"Still I'm scared," I said. "He's a bully, isn't he?"

"He won't dare touch you," he assured me.

"Maybe," I said. "I don't know really. Can you beat him
in a fight?"

"How would I know?" he said irritably.

But I knew he couldn't beat Jester.

However, Milton was right in his assurances that Jester
wouldn't molest me. I met Jester after that, not while I had
the fishpot, but one evening when I had gone to the shop.
And he didn't blacken my eye. He didn't touch me. He didn't
even say anything about the morning that I had refused to
show him what I had caught in the pot.

But strange things began to happen. The pot ceased to catch
any fish, and this went on for days, until Milton made a
startling discovery one morning. He had just returned from
attending the animals in the field when he took a look at the
pot where I had, in disgust, thrown it.

"You pulled the bung out?" he asked me.

He was referring to the ball of thrash we used to cork the
exit of the pot while it was in the water.

"No," I said. "I haven't touched anything."

"It wasn't like that when I corked it yesterday evening,"
he said.

"What do you mean?" I asked.

"Somebody has interfered with it."

"Somebody? What somebody?"

"Look. Whoever corked it up again did it in a hurry or
did it carelessly."

Which was true, because the thrash was not balled neatly and parts of it hung loose.

"Meaning," Milt went on, "that someone has been playing us tricks. Watching where we set the pot and drawing it in the mornings before you get to it. Then setting it back in the water as if nothing had happened."

"So that's why we don't catch fish anymore!"

"Exactly," Milt said. "That somebody takes the fish out before you get there."

"What'll we do now?" I wanted to know.

"Set a watch and catch him."

"And if we catch him?"

"We'll do something about it," he said.

"Something like what? I'd like to get my hands on him."

I was mad that somebody could have been doing this to us and so making us have to eat more codfish than was necessary—and spend money to buy it.

The next morning Milton and I woke a bit before dawn and went down to the river where we had put in the pot the previous evening. There was fog lying in the valley and it looked like a swab of cotton and the trees lacked sharp outlines in the thin darkness. We squatted in a clump of shrubs and waited. That someone who was drawing our pot couldn't have been earlier than us. We didn't have to wait long either before our quarry came along. And who was that quarry? Thank you very much: that's as good a guess as any I have ever heard.

Jester indeed!

He was sure of himself, sure that he was minutes ahead of me, because he didn't waste time with such preliminaries as looking around him for anyone. He proceeded immediately to draw the pot. We allowed him to do so and to pull the bung out.

Then Milton said, "*Drop* it!"

Sure he was frightened, this Jester, at being caught red-handed, but he wasn't the one to run. He did not drop the pot either, but when Milton and I stood up and walked out of our hiding place, Jester's face underwent a change. Fright changed into belligerence on that round dirty face.

"Who you talkin' to?" he asked.

"You," Milton said, walking toward him. "That pot is not yours. You are a thief!"

"You callin' *me* a thief?"

"Yes," Milton said. "You are a sneak-thief."

This I considered strong language for Milton to use to Jester, because he was no match for the bully. Milton was thirteen and Jester, if anything, must have been fifteen and going on sixteen.

To understand Jester's power one would have to have a knowledge of his capacity. He wasn't called Jester because he was a joker or a comedian. No, he got his name from a special kind of pot called a jester pot. The story went that the bully had eaten off, in a single go, all the yam boiled in a full jester pot that boasted a six-man capacity. Since this feat he had been nicknamed Jester.

But the fact that Jester was a champion eater also meant that he was strong. He must have beaten up nine out of every ten boys in Boswell at some time or another. No one playing a game with Jester could win. What I mean is, if he won, he'd still be beaten up and, knowing this, he purposely lost to Jester to spare himself. A boy could get beaten up by just looking at Jester, who would say, "Hey! What you lookin' at me for?" And he'd proceed to hit the boy. Some boys, knowing this, took steps not to look at him, but this didn't save them from the almighty Jester. He'd demand to know what was the matter with him, why he wasn't looked at, and he'd start throwing punches even before he got an answer.

Jester was the most well-fed boy in all Boswell because so many boys paid him hands-off dues in the form of food. I had seen many a boy give up his choicest fruit to Jester as a peace-offering. So I was more than surprised to hear Milton talking to Jester in such harsh terms.

He would fight, as I expected.

He made fists and came at Milton and the latter went on guard to meet the challenge. Jester got in a few early blows and, frankly, I feared greatly for Milton; but Jester had never learned to organize anything, not even his strength. Milton, skipping around nimbly, avoided most of his sledge-hammer blows. Soon Jester was snorting from weariness, and the fact that his punches were not going home seemed to madden him and he rushed at Milton wildly. But he didn't demolish Milton, who now began to go on to the offensive, getting in a punch or two of his own. Milton's face was blazing with concentration and I cheered him on.

"Hit him, Milt! Hit him!"

Though Milton was bleeding in the nose, he was landing a few punches. He put down one on Jester's ear and it went red, and then he got another into his mouth and the foolish Jester went off guard to spit and determine if he had lost a tooth or sustained a cut mouth. Milton got an opportunity to demolish his opponent and he made ample use of it at that. He let loose with a trio of swift blockblusters—one to the stomach, another whammed into Jester's right cheek, and the third found a landing place in the left eye. Jester squirmed and covered his eye with one hand and, excited now by his success, Milton continued to rain blows on his opponent. In the head, on the neck, on the point of the chin . . . wham! and wham! and

wham! The bully could take no more. He turned and showed
us a pair of dew-wet heels as he skimmed away.

"How'd you do it?" I asked, as if I hadn't seen how all right.

"The thief!" Milt said.

"Your nose is bleeding," I said.

"I fixed him," Milt said, wiping blood from his nose.

"He ran faster'n a race horse," I said.

The pot had caught an interminably long eel, black and
sleek. He was big too and flip-flapped his tail in the pot.

"Look what he would have got," Milt said.

"And to think of what he must have got since he started his tricks," I said.

"His thefts," Milton said. "His thefts, you mean."

Milton went down into the water and washed the blood away from his nose and we went home, carrying the eel along in the pot. We didn't tell Grandpa what happened.

Milton killed the eel and cleaned it and it was hung high in the kitchen beams so that the smoke could cure it. When it was all cured we ate it fried and even Grandpa commented on the quality of the meat. It had fed us three, but Jester would have eaten it all off at a single sitting and gotten fat at our expense.

We had no more trouble from Jester after that, and he was even desperate in his efforts to get on friendly terms with Milton. The word got around, too—mainly through me—that Jester had been nailed, and he was less the bully.

There wasn't much we could do with what money we were saving, but Milton sometimes thought of getting Grandpa a wooden leg made, though he wasn't certain that that would have gotten him to church again. Things were going better, however. Milton was the man of the house and he controlled the money that came in from the scanty produce we sold, and also what went out to buy us necessities. Of course, he talked things over with Grandpa, who only gave his consent in the form of a grunted Uh-huh, but offered no criticism.

Soon Red Gal was heavy with calf, and her udder had filled with milk and the teats grown taut. She was expected to have calf at any time and even Grandpa showed some interest in the coming event by asking Milt every morning after his return from the fields if the calf was born. Pal Joe, too, had grown into quite a sassy young thing and was fleet of foot. Milt's goats were fine too. The kid was healthy and stocky of body. But the most important animal was Red Gal. We all knew that she would play an important role in our economy.

I had started to accompany Milton to the fields in the mornings, because we suspected that Red Gal would give birth at night and I wished to see the calf as early as possible. But with all my efforts I didn't succeed. One morning I overslept. When I awoke Milton wasn't there in the bed beside me and I knew he had dressed and gone to the fields. I got out of bed, dressed hastily as a fireman, and made a dash out of the house. But I got only as far as the front yard. Milton was coming toward the house full tilt and he was hollering his head off, so that even Allan Bent opened a window and looked out.

"The calf is born!" he was saying.

Grandpa came out of his sleep slowly.

"Eh?"

"A—calf—Grandpa," Milt said. He was breathing so hard that it interfered with his speech.

"Bull or heifer?" Grandpa asked, sitting up.

"I . . . I . . ."

That was it. He had not gone to the trouble of finding that out. Who would have, anyway? But he would find out now in his second dash to where Red Gal was quartered. And I was with him this time. I hoisted a hand to Allan as we dashed out.

Ordinarily Milton can outrun me, but because I was now the fresher of the two, I held my place right by his heels—along the track, then through the dew-wet grass, across the footbridge over the river, and then we were there.

Red Gal was lanky-bellied now like a bag that had gone empty, and she was walking around and uttering things in her throat. The calf was brown in color and stood tall on wobbly legs. It was learning to walk but stumbling badly, and its mother was right by it every way it turned, licking it with her flicking tongue. I stood there looking on in wonder until Milton said happily, "Isn't he beautiful?"

I had to agree. "But is he a he?" I asked.

"I haven't found out yet," Milton admitted.

We were standing a good way away and were forced to do so because Red Gal looked menacing and mean and meant to have her calf to herself. She was still uttering things in her throat and watching us and flicking her head belligerently when she wasn't giving her baby a bath with her tongue. The calf required milk and staggered along its mother's side and found the udder all right without trouble. It got on to a teat, too, which was as fat as a sausage but a lot stiffer.

We edged around Red Gal, who continued to moo in her throat, until we finally found that her calf was a bull.

"What will you call him?" I asked.

"Call him?"

"The calf. Aren't you going to give him a *name*?"

"Yes, but I haven't thought of it yet."

"Well, think now," I said.

"Yes. But first, I'll give Red Gal something fresh to eat."

With Red Gal acting the way she was, Milton didn't think it a safe thing to try to tether her elsewhere, so he proceeded to cut down, with his cutlass, three bamboo trees from a grove which grew nearby. He dragged the first within reach of Red Gal, then he carried another, and the third. I didn't help him. I was safe where I stood and had no wish to go nearer.

The calf wasn't sucking now, and Red Gal walked toward the juicy leaves. The calf stumbled tall-legged beside her and took a sniff at the leaves, but turned away. It was then that Allan Bent walked on to the scene. He was smoking his pipe and he wore his trouser legs stuffed down into his knee-high rubber boots.

"Look, Allan," I said. "The calf."

"So I see," Allan said, removing his pipe.

Milton said, "He's a bull."

"Fine."

"Milton doesn't know what he's going to call him," I said.

"It takes time to find a name," Allan said.

"But he could have had a name ready," I argued.

Milton growled at me and went off to look after Pal Joe and his goats. Allan and I stood there and talked.

"When are we going to start milking?" I asked.

"Four weeks from now," Allan said.

"Four! Why four?"

" 'Cause we want to give that calf a good start," Allan said, preparing himself for a lecture. "The milk is his, y'know. When we take milk from the mother, we only rob him. It's like this, Timmy. When a baby's born, he can't eat bread and things like us, so he lives on milk mostly, his mother's milk, until he can partake o' things like us. Things like bread and rice and meat and yams. It's the same with that there calf. He got to have the milk until he gets stronger before we start robbin' him o' what's his . . ."

Allan spat on the grass and went on.

"Of course, not all cows allow their calves to suck the milk for any time. I hear that the thoroughbred cows like the Jersey don't. Soon after the calf is born the mother, I understand, won't have nothin' to do with it. So somebody got to feed it with milk. The common breed cows, like Red Gal, are different. The calf can stay for months until weaned."

"What's a thoroughbred cow, Allan?" I asked.

"Them's cows that got class. Them's high-class cows."

"They sound like foolish cows to me," I said.

We saw Milton returning.

The sun had come over the hill and dew was glinting on the grass and leaves. I could see that Milton had been walking in tall grass because his legs were wet and even the bottom of his shorts were damp.

I gave him no time and as soon as he had joined us I asked, "What are you going to call him, Milt?"

"Buster, maybe," he said.

"*Buster!* What for?"

"I don't know what for," he said. "But I think I'll call him that."

I turned to Allan. "Did you ever hear of a cow called Buster, Allan?"

"Doncher like it?" Allan asked me. "Buster sounds all right to me. Doncher like it?"

"Yes," I said. "Maybe I do. A name's a name, isn't it, Allan? 'Bye, Buster," I said to the calf, before we walked away.

··{4}··
A Plan for Christmas

It was mid-November. Riggan, the butcher, was out by two weeks. He had said the calf would have arrived in December, but the calf was two weeks early. And so much the better. Its coming was like the leap of a flame in the darkness. Everybody was lighthearted, as if a problem had been solved. Milton, me, Allan Bent, even Grandpa—each morning he asked Milton about the calf and each afternoon as well. It seemed as if the calf had given him some hope, because he didn't look so sad as he used to and his beardy chin was seen less on his breast than before. To liven him up some more Milton even led the cow home with Buster following behind, so Grandpa could get acquainted with him. Buster pranced about the yard with his tail high, much to Grandpa's delight.

"Watch him gallivantin'," Grandpa said. "Great Jehoso-phat, what a lovely calf!"

Allan and Milton were getting things organized for the

sale of the milk. We bought a milk pan made of tin and having a turncock spout in the side near its bottom. At its top was a handle made of strong wire and this made it easy for the pan to be slung from the hand. Allan and Milton had found customers too. I gathered from their discussion that Mister Lethbridge, the proprietor of the large general store, would take a quart each day; and Miss Pinkerton, the postmistress, a pint; and Victor Lassy, who was a foreman in the area for the Public Works Department, would require another pint a day. There were a couple of others whose names I did not get. I soon learned the part I was to play: deliver to the regular customers, leaving Milton free to undertake a house-to-house selling campaign, supplying housewives and mothers with a pint or a half-pint according to their needs.

We had ample time to get ourselves prepared for the milk-selling drive, which, fortunately, could begin before Christmas and provide some well-needed cash. School was finished and the Christmas holidays had begun.

Now every boy in Boswell cultivated an interest in vehicles. If on an errand we came upon a sugar-cane truck or other vehicle disabled for any reason or having a punctured tire changed, we remained rooted to the spot, watching what the men were doing, listening to their language, picking up such words as "gear-teeth," "lugs," and "carburetor." We never remembered the errand until, its repair done, the truck left the spot, or somebody carrying a switch came to see what was keeping us. We simply adored machines. Mister Chaney, the big man in Boswell, had a car, and we'd pray for a heavy shower of rain to fall whenever the car was out. Then, on returning, it would skid on its way up the hill to the house, and anybody at hand—man, woman, or child—would rush to help push the car until the wheels found a grip.

A number of us boys at some time or another owned toy vehicles we had fashioned as trucks. Some boasted cabs made out of tin and bodies put together with board. Others were merely carts pushed by hand. Mine was one such vehicle, and I set about repairing a broken wheel and converting it slightly so that I could make use of it in milk delivery. I got two strips of board cut and asked Mister Romney, one of the local carpenters, to saw circular holes down their center. Each strip of board thus accommodated six holes, every one of a size to hold a milk bottle. These strips were then nailed down on my cart in such a way that I could stack two rows of bottles. And then I was ready.

The longest four weeks I ever experienced came to an end and it was time for us to start robbing Buster of his milk. Allan promised he would help initiate Red Gal into the business of milking. He was there on time, too, to get things going and also, I suspected, to help put Red Gal into a co-operative frame of mind. But Red Gal was very co-operative, anyway. She was tethered short to a tree and, of course, not being accustomed to having fingers grab and pull at her teats, she shied away a couple of times while Allan attempted to wash down her udder and teats.

Buster was raging in the little pen constructed for him and in which he had spent the night so that he couldn't get at the milk. He was all agog for it, but he couldn't get over the wooden rails nor between them. He was a spruce young fellow by now, chubby and all that, and his legs were no longer tall and frail. Now he moved on them with assurance, as he turned this way and that and pushed his hornless head between the rails and trumpeted his baby moos.

"Wait awhile, Buster," I said. "We won't take all the milk, boy. Be patient, Buster. We'll help ourselves to some and leave yours. Calm down, friend, just one minute now."

But he didn't understand me and, even if he could have, I doubt if he would have accepted advice. He was accustomed to waking at dawn and persuading his mother to stand so that he could have breakfast—and this was well past the time.

Red Gal's udder was full of milk and, with the teats taut, it hung like a pot with four legs.

Soon Allan had washed the udder and teats clean and began milking. He was cautious and refused to rest the pan on the ground and milk with both hands into it. Red Gal, he said, was still jumpy and could overturn the pan. So Allan milked

with one hand, holding a mug with another. He was milking into the mug. The milk came out of the teat in a straight slant line like a white cord and chirped musically as it hit the bottom of the mug. Then the sound grew muffled as the milk rose in the mug. There was a cap of thick froth on the top and, when the mug was full, Allan tipped the contents into the pan. And we were under way.

Allan didn't milk the udder dry but left some for Buster. After all, it was his milk. The moment he was released from his pen he made a beeline for the teats, but by then they were no longer taut with ready milk. They were flabby and Buster set to work, knocking the udder up with his forehead a couple of times, then settling down to sucking, moving from teat to teat, the milk foaming at the corners of his mouth. His wagging tail was very indicative of his pleasure. Red Gal was indifferent. She chewed her cud.

We didn't attempt to sell all the six quarts of milk. We set aside some for our needs, and Allan Bent got a pint from time to time. The rest was sold, and at the end of the week we found we hadn't done badly for a first week. We had collected fifteen shillings. Fifteen! That was money we hadn't seen in a long time. The milk had turned out to be white gold! Even Grandpa must have seen the possibilities ahead. He smacked his lips and said, "Drat. You boys got off to a doggoned good start. Better'n I expected. You made money I never dreamed you'd make."

I would have betted my week's supply of milk that Grandpa was taking heart again.

Meanwhile, Christmas was upon us. It was but a week away.

In Boswell at that time, you could feel Christmas coming. The air was cooler now and brisker, and Christmas was also visible. Plants seemed to vie one with the other in flowering for Christmas. The sugar cane did its part in decorating the countryside. It still does. At Christmas it produces its flower (if it can be called a flower), which we call its arrow because of the likeness. Newly arrived, this arrow is crowded with downy tassels, but as the shaft pushes up and the arrow loses its youth, the tassels vanish slowly. The sugar-cane fields are a beauty to see at Christmastime, covering wide acres of flat land. The arrows stand, hundreds together, like great armies of archers.

As Christmas approached, people began to put away money for the big day, and almost every household had its fatted pig or goat or rooster, the pig or goat or rooster that would adorn the Christmas platter and stuff the stomachs. People shook out their moneybags to eat their best, to wear the gaudiest clothes, and to buy for Christmas in the shops and at the fairs.

If the children hadn't saved any money during the year, this was the time when they tried to find something at least to sell and so make some money. This could be something growing wild, such as ginger. It could be something cultivated, such as yam. It could be a chicken, which someone in a nearby village or town would buy for his dinner or for keeping to raise a brood. It could be a dozen eggs; and some boys even managed to have a goat for sale.

Placards appeared on shop walls and on trees and on moving vehicles. They told of the annual fair that would be held on the Boswell Cricket Grounds on Christmas Day. In this year of which I am writing, it was planned to be a real bang-up affair. There was going to be a visiting team of cricketers playing against the Boswell Eleven, and instead of local musicians, who were guitarists, a drummer, and fife players, there was going to be an orchestra from the town of Lucea! At this fair there would be maypole dancing. There would also be shoot-

ing, and the prize was to be a giant ham. There would be dancing and attractions galore.

Milton and I soon discovered that with our thoughts centered on Grandpa we had been caught napping. We were hopelessly unprepared for Christmas. To make it worse, Milton
had taken to spending most of his leisure hours with Margaret
Chaney.

Margaret was the only child of the Chaneys. She was formerly Milton's classmate at Boswell, but her father's money had
taken her out of the local school and whisked her away to a
secondary school in Kingston. Home for the holidays, she had
not forgotten Milton. Together they roamed the countryside
in search of what Margaret called specimens. They collected
frogs among the reeds in the river and butterflies and other
specimens in the woodlands.

Margaret was good company. She was a nice girl. What
I mean is, she was kind and all that. If she was eating a candy
and saw you, you wouldn't have to look candy-minded for
her to break it and give you a half. She was nice right through,
good looking and all, and she was the only girl in Boswell who
could ride a horse better than most boys.

But for all this I didn't see much sense in going around with
Milton and her and wasting time collecting frogs and butterflies and gathering ferns and flowers and whatnot. Sometimes
I went to the river with them and up to the Great House too,
but there I usually found something to tinker with, or I'd
help Freddy, the handyman, to wash the car. When I was
tired of being at the Great House I went into the fields and
watched the men at work, and if the tractor was working, so
much the better.

So Milton and I fooled around a lot in those first two weeks
of holidays. And the result? We had completely forgotten

about Christmas, and we were hopelessly unprepared.

I didn't find out how much this meant until one morning, on returning from the milk delivery, I saw Onis on the road. Onis was a short boy, short and stocky and with no sign that he would ever be much taller than his four foot one. He had a heart-shaped face and a set of good white teeth in his mouth, which was a bit on the wide side whenever he grinned; and it was often that Onis grinned. He walked around with a ready smile for his friends, and he was so conscious of his muscles that he wore his short sleeves rolled high on his upper arms and the legs of his shorts were even turned up a few folds so that his thigh muscles could be on display. Onis lived about three houses away from me.

"Hey, Timmy," he greeted me.

"What's up, Onis?" I slashed back.

He fixed his hands akimbo. That was another thing Onis was always doing—fixing his hands akimbo.

"The fair on Christmas Day, Timmy," he said. "It's driving me crazy. I want to have all the money I can lay my hands on. I'm going to need pocketfuls of money, Timmy, for that fair."

"Yes," I said, without much warmth or enthusiasm, realizing how unprepared I was for this fair, Christmas, everything. Other years I had saved money; I had stored things to sell. This year nothing. Grandpa's accident had knocked everything askew.

"Wouldn't you like to have a lot of money?" he asked, grinning.

"Sure," I said.

"You sounded at first as if you weren't interested," Onis said.

"Who, me? Of course I'm interested."

"Oh." Now he shifted his weight to one foot. Many people

thought and said that Onis would grow to become Boswell's top boaster when he matured and mellowed. He did cut a good figure standing there, hands on his hips, weight on one foot.

"I'm planning to sell my two fowls," he went on. "Ma has agreed, even. I've got the pullet tied up already. She weighs two and a half pounds. But the rooster—he's giving me no end of trouble."

"What trouble?"

"To catch. He doesn't sleep at our place any more. He's adopted the yard next to ours. He sleeps at Josh Tingling's. I guess it's because there are more hens there than at my place. You know the mango tree in Josh's backyard, don't you?"

I knew it. Josh and Onis lived near.

"Well, that's where that rooster sleeps at night."

"Maybe you'll have to surprise him while he's still asleep on his roost," I suggested.

"Maybe," Onis said. "Maybe I'll have to get there while it's still dark tomorrow morning and climb into that tree and nab the scoundrel."

"Do that," I encouraged him.

"Fact is, I'm getting impatient with that rooster, Timmy. I want to have the money in my hands. You ever been impatient?" he said and offered another grin.

"Me? Sure," I told him. "But waiting another day to nab that rooster isn't too long a wait."

"Maybe," he said. "Maybe."

There was a desperate longing in his eyes as I moved away, and I was feeling miserable as a fish out of water.

His trouble with his rooster didn't surprise me one bit, however. In Boswell few people kept their fowls shut in. It was usual for the birds to be left running about in the daytime, and they'd keep on the premises to which they belonged or go wandering off a bit. They came home in the afternoons for food and to their roosts, but there were always some delinquents, usually young roosters. They disliked roosting in their own yards, as if roosting at home made them sissies. Make no mistake about roosters: they are just as proud and vain as men and boys.

I had one such delinquent bird, a pullet. She was so unruly and mischievous that I had nicknamed her Trouble.

I went home, racking my brains in an effort to come up with a way of making some money for Christmas. I had neglected gathering ginger. I had no kind of produce I could sell. Milton, I realized, was in a far better position than I. He had a goat-kid. He could have it sold if he had a mind to. I had nothing. I'd have to think of something though. Maybe Trouble. Maybe I'd be obliged to catch her and sell her. She wouldn't fetch much money, but it would be better than no money at all. I kept the idea alive in my head.

As I suspected, Onis's impatience had gotten the better of him and he was in no waiting mood. No sooner had I gotten home than I heard a racket near our house and, looking out, I saw Onis full tilt after the rooster, a beautiful white bird if ever there was one. But, as Onis closed in on it, the wise bird took to its wings.

I thought I'd give Onis a hand and told Milton so. I joined Onis in the open lot. The rooster was intelligent and had hidden wherever it had landed after its flight, because I found Onis completely baffled. He and I had a conference.

"What do you think?" he asked. "Where could he have gone?"

"Not far," I said.

"But where? He's resting, see? Wherever he is he's resting. Then he'll be fresh again to run. The scoundrel."

We beat down the grass all around, but there was no rooster. Then we looked toward a patch of pineapple plants growing nearby. This was an ideal place for a fowl to hide, what with the prickles with which the pineapple plants arm themselves.

"He must be in there," I said.

"You bet," Onis agreed.

But it wasn't easy to get him. We tried searching the pineapple patch, but soon we were getting prickles buried in our flesh. Pineapple plants planted and cared for are kept in rows, but this was a deserted patch and the plants had clustered and grown over each other and there was no pathway between them any more.

Then I had an idea.

"Wait a minute," I said, and ran back to the house.

Champion was asleep, but he woke up and yawned with a yipe as I approached. I untied his chain and he was happy to be going somewhere. He ran on before me as if he sensed some adventure ahead, but I held him with the leash. He was whining and eager, and I said, "Give us a hand, Champ. Get him, boy."

He barked and strained on the leash.

This was all that was necessary. His barks and whines unsettled the rooster, who must have sensed danger. Out of the middle of the pineapples he flew and Onis was after him in a flash. I knew better than to let Champion in on the chase. He had a love for fowls that I couldn't trust. So I tied the leash to a shrub and joined Onis in the pursuit.

Fully rested, the rooster was running like mad. He soon took to flight again and pitched into a tree, but we scared him out and ran beneath him as he skimmed in a slant into a banana field. He was tired now and was slowing up. Onis lunged forward, and threw out his arms. The race was over.

The captured rooster squawked like mad and, hearing this, Champion barked excitedly.

"Got him," Onis said, with Onis-type glee.

"He's all yours," I said.

Onis stood and weighed the bird in his hand.

"About six pounds," he said.

I took the bird and risked a guess.

"To me he's nearer five than six."

"What's a pound's difference?" Onis said. "At a shilling a pound at this time of year, and five or six pounds . . . that's at least five shillings."

"Good money," I said.

"And there's the pullet," Onis pointed out. "Both of them will bring in near eight shillings and I have two-and-six-pence in my savings. Remember?" He laughed the Onis laugh, showing his gleaming white teeth.

"You're a millionaire," I said miserably.

"You bet. I'll have a good time at Christmas."

"You certainly will, Onis," I said.

"Thanks," he said, walking away with his squawking rooster. "I'll be seeing you."

"It wasn't any trouble to help," I said dejectedly.

Walking back, I untied Champion from the shrub. His excitement was still running high and he was uttering yipe after yipe, but I led him back to the house.

Before I could join Milton in the kitchen, up came Cal Symes into the yard. As if my sorrows were not already enough.

Cal lived on a ridge near to ours and he had only to run down to the valley that separated us and up the hill to get to our house. Cal had done it so often getting to our place, and

I had done it so often getting to his place, that our feet had beaten out a track. Cal no longer went by the usual pathway from their house to the village square. He used the track that our feet had made, and cutting across our yard, he was on the road in no time.

Cal was on his way to the village.

"What you got there, Cal?" I asked him. He was carrying a parcel and was holding it fondly as a woman would caress a baby. He patted the paper parcel before he answered me. So I took a pat too. Whatever it was, the stuff felt gravelly to me.

"What is it?" I asked.

"Ginger," Cal said.

"Your own?"

"Who else's?"

I had nothing to say.

"Where's yours?" he asked me.

"None," was all I said.

"You have *none*?"

Which was surprising to me too, because I always had ginger dried and stored some place for the lucrative Christmas market.

"No," I said, feeling like Boswell's official fool. "I've got none, Cal."

"You must be joking or something?"

"No, Cal," I said.

At any time whatsoever, ginger commanded top price, but at Christmastime it was at its peak. Only pimento as a produce, pound for pound, was perhaps as valuable. Ginger was usually cultivated, but also grew wild in the woodlands. Children went searching for it and dug up the tubers, scraped the skin away, and dried it. Mister Lethbridge, the proprietor of the general store, traded in agricultural produce and bought ginger. He stored what he bought and sold bagfuls at a time to a merchant in Kingston. Cal was now on his way to Mister Lethbridge's store.

The year before I had sold four pounds of ginger and had gotten seven shillings for it. Now I had none. Very funny indeed. Grandpa's accident certainly had played havoc with our normal procedures. We were two boys caught napping.

"This is about seven pounds," Cal said and grinned. I was lucky he couldn't grin quite as wide as Onis.

"You'll be rich," I said. "Seven one-and-ninepences . . . Wow!"

"Not too much for me to spend though," he said. "I'll need it at the fair. It's going to be quite a fair."

Yes, the fair, the fair. It was going to be quite a fair. A bang-up affair. A hallelujah kind of fair. A moneyless one for me.

"So long," he said.

"I'll be seeing you," I said.

He took a couple of steps then he stopped and turned, his face now as serious as a judge's.

"D'you really mean you've no ginger to sell, Timmy?"

"I mean it," I said.

"Cross your heart," Cal demanded.

Instead I said, "As the Lord liveth, Cal."

When a boy said this it was taken that he was speaking the truth and nothing but the truth. You couldn't associate the Lord's name with a lie. All sorts of bad things could happen to you if you did; you could drop dead, people said. So Cal believed. He shrugged his shoulders and looked at me with eyes full of pity.

He went on down our hill, clutching his parcel of ginger lovingly to his side. I looked long after him and I felt so miserable I wanted to cry. I felt like a balloon with no air in it.

"Don't worry," said a voice beside me.

I turned. It was Milton's. He had joined me and I hadn't even noticed.

"Don't worry, Timmy. We didn't make any preparations but we aren't too late," he said.

This, to me, seemed like thoroughbred nonsense, but it also represented hope. I grabbed at it—I was ready to grab at anything.

"What d'you mean, not too late?" I asked.

"I mean we can plan to make some money."

"By selling milk?"

"No," he said, landing a hand on my shoulder. "Not by selling milk."

"You must be crazy," I said.

"I'm not either."

He wasn't looking at me but away toward the hills in the distance, and I didn't think he was looking at anything up there either. His brows were furrowed and his eyes narrowed and his profile rugged and—jeez!—he looked like a man.

"Real money?" I asked. "We're going to make real money?"

"Sure. What do you mean, real money?"

I knew what I meant all right, because, I didn't see how we were going to make money from nothing. We had nothing we could sell. Nothing. But Milton, it seemed, knew better.

"Of course, we won't have much money before Christmas Day . . ." he went on.

This didn't seem too good to me, but I waited.

". . . But we could have a pile by the end of Christmas Day."

"The end you say? When all the fun is over?" Who wanted a pile of money when there was nothing to be done with it?

Then Milton laid his plan before me and I realized that in a scheme like that I could have more fun than from just spending money. Moreover this thing we were going to embark on could bring Grandpa happiness. And that was the best part.

"There's going to be this big fair," Milton said, his hands deep in his pockets now, "and there'll be several stalls run by different people. So why don't we run one too? It's my idea, but Margaret has helped me work it out."

So running around with Margaret, collecting specimens, did bear some fruit!

"I've already asked permission from Miss Raymond, who is on the committee," he went on. "This is the way I've got it figured, Timmy. Suppose we make enough money—four pounds, five, ten, even—depending on how much we put into it . . ."

Yes, how much we put into it, I thought. You can't expect much in profit unless you pump a lot in as outlay. And what had we?

". . . We could do a lot. I've been toying with an idea. I thought at first that with Pal Joe growing up we could use the profits and buy Grandpa a saddle so that he could ride around—go anywhere he wishes, but to church, mostly. We know how much he wants to get back to church. Well, if we make the right kind of money at the fair, couldn't we go a step further and, with milk sales improving, get a little buggy instead and a horse to draw it?"

"A buggy!"

"Sure. Don't you know a buggy?"

Sure I knew a buggy—a kind of fancy cart. But this seemed too big a deal for us.

"Mister Vincent, the wheelwright at Johnson Corner, has an old buggy. Maybe with repairs it could be put on the road again. We could buy it and a horse to draw it."

"That's great," I said. "But can we do it? I mean run a good stall and make that kind of money?"

"That's what we're aiming to do," Milt said. "We made fifteen shillings from milk sales last week. We hope to make at least that amount this week too, or do better. That'll be thirty shillings at least. My goat has a kid six months old now—"

"You're going to sell him?" I interrupted. It was a fine young he-goat and was growing rapidly.

"No," Milton said. "I'll do better than sell him. Why, if I have him butchered, he'll yield enough meat to cook a whopping good goat's flesh curry to put on sale. And at a shilling a plate . . ."

Goodness, Milton was indeed thinking big!

"Let's go into the kitchen," he said, and I followed him. He went on preparing breakfast as he talked, and I soon learned that in our cellar he had stored a total of five dry coconuts, and he also had an eye on a matured bunch that was still on a tree. These to make coconut cakes.

"Well," I said. "Who'll do the baking?" We had no oven, no knowhow.

"That's where Margaret comes in."

"Can she bake?"

"A little. But there's her mother to help."

"Do you mean you've asked Mrs. Chaney to help?" I asked.

"Why not? You know Mrs. Chaney. Always happy to help."

"Great Jehosophat!" I said.

"I talked it over with Margaret and told her how Grandpa had become grumpy and sad and was not really alive. I told her what I'd like to do for him and she talked it over with her mother. Her mother went to Mister Chaney with it and then both of them, the elder Chaneys, wanted to give Grandpa a buggy for Christmas, but I would have none of it. And you know very well, too, that Grandpa would have none of that."

"I know," I said. "We Cassidys can be proud."

"I told Mrs. Chaney that their help would be all I needed and, besides, it would be fun for us to get this done ourselves."

"And she agreed?"

"Yes. Margaret will help her with the baking, and we will too, by providing the firewood for the oven and such."

"That's no trouble," I said. "When is the baking to be?"

"Monday. Christmas Eve."

"And the cooking?"

"Christmas Day. Early in the day. That will be Allan's job. He's wonderful at currying."

"But shall we have enough money for all this?" I asked.

"Yes. We may well have. There's the thirty shillings. And if that's not enough, we could borrow from Mrs. Chaney and repay her from the profits."

"Oh, boy," I said. "I'm beginning to like this."

Milton sweetened Grandpa's coffee and our chocolate and began to slice the bread.

"We need eggs. We have only seven now. At most we can hope to have another six by Monday, if the hens go on laying. But we'll need a dozen and a half more."

"We'll have to buy," I said.

"Yes. Maybe. But I hate to spend money on things like eggs. I mean, we ought to save money on things we can produce for ourselves."

"Yes. That would be good, Milt."

He left me then to take Grandpa his breakfast. But he left me fired with enthusiasm. This was a big operation and it tickled me that three of us—Margaret, he, and I—would or could accomplish something that only adults were expected to accomplish and which only they had so far ever attempted. Whoever heard of children running a stall at the fair?

·{5}·
Gains and Losses

Milton said we were short of eggs, and the fact that I had helped Onis catch his wayward rooster set me thinking about my delinquent pullet, Trouble. She had been a trouble-maker from early in her life and throughout it, flying up where she was not wanted and breaking earthenware plates and cups and saucers in the act. Like Onis's rooster, she didn't roost on her own premises. For some time I had suspected that she was laying, but hadn't bothered to find out where. Now that we were short of eggs I thought seriously of doing a bit of detective work on her. If indeed she were laying in some hidden place —in a cozy nest she had made in a field, a patch of grass, or under a hedge—there'd be eggs.

"I think maybe Trouble is laying," I said to Milton.

"How d'you know?" he asked.

"When you see her next, look at her comb. It's bright red. And I've heard her cackling a couple of times."

"So watch her," Milt said. "Keep an eye on her. Find out where she goes. And most important of all, find out where she comes from when she cackles."

"That's some job," I said, not minding it one bit.

"It will be worth it," Milt said.

At this time we had few fowls. Our birds had been destroyed by mongooses. The mongoose, not so common now as in those days, had been imported into Jamaica from India or thereabouts to kill off the snakes. Let loose, and having multiplied, and being efficient in the job of killing snakes, the mongoose soon had nothing to do for a pastime and little more to eat in the way of snake-steaks. So he turned his meat-loving attention to the island's poultry, which went freely about the yards. Our flocks of birds had been decimated by the mongoose. Of course these attacks on them had taken place before Champion became a member of our household. A dog is the greatest enemy of the mongoose and, with Champion in our yard, no mongoose would have had the spunk to enter it and molest our birds.

"If what you suspect about Trouble is right," Milton said, "we'll have more eggs and we won't have to buy extra, maybe."

"Right," I said with some enthusiasm. "I'll watch her. I'll follow that Trouble and nab her."

"A pity you can't do it today," he said. "But we have to go to the hills for grass to fill the mattresses."

I liked going to the hills for grass. There wasn't anyone around who wasted money on buying new mattresses, when he could go to the hills and cut what we called "bed-grass." By Christmas this was dry and shiny and silky to the touch and, using knives, we cut it and carried it home stuffed into bags. We sunned it some more in our yards and then it was ready for the mattresses. And fine mattresses it made, too.

We were going to give ourselves new mattresses for Christmas, and this meant going to the hills. So I couldn't have kept a watch on Trouble that day.

This watching of Trouble was going to be fun, though. It wasn't often that a boy got the chance of doing a little shadowing, even if his quarry turned out to be a pullet with bad habits. So I looked forward to it.

That night I was so tired that I dropped off to sleep almost immediately after diving into bed. Milton also. At some time in the night I woke up and heard rain falling—torrential rain. The raindrops were big and shelled the roof like pellets, and the lightning flicked at the glass windows like something's tongue, and the thunder was like an old man grumbling. A storm such as this was unusual for December, but who cared? Not me. Beside me Milton was sound asleep and the rhythmic drumming of raindrops returned me to blissful sleep too.

It seemed the rain had fallen all night because, when we awoke, we heard the river belly-full with water and when I looked out of the window, I saw it dirt-colored and lively, rushing along. The plants around, especially sugar cane and bananas, had a whipped appearance as if they had taken an awful beating. Some sugar cane, too tall to be sturdy, had fallen flat, and the large feather-shaped banana leaves were torn to shreds. And not only that: some mature plants with fruit on them had been blown flat to the ground.

The moment Milton saw all this his face flared up.

"Omigosh!" he said. "The fishpot."

Fool that I was, I had not thought of the fishpot! Even on its leash it could never have survived this flood. Not with the river brimful with water that rushed along like a great gray snake. Yet we hoped—hoped that it hadn't been washed far;

that, broken from its leash, it had tangled with rocks and had been saved; had perhaps been washed completely onto a bank; or was miraculously covered up in the bottom of the pool by sand from upstream. Covered up and saved before the flood-water had really assaulted it in full force. But, as we looked at the water, even now that the rain that fed it had stopped, and listening to its bellicose sounds, we knew, Milton and I, that our hopes were slender.

No more fish. No more eels. And crayfish soup had become a household word to us and eel steak held a place on our table. Their loss would be by no means comforting.

"Funny to have rain like this so close to Christmas," Grandpa said, looking out from the veranda. "Look at that river prancing with water!" Then he must have read the anxiety on our faces.

"You didn't set that fishpot, did you?" he asked Milton.

"Er . . . yes, Grandpa."

"Same thing I said. That river always takes them fishpots. Every year the same thing." Then he smiled curiously as he lit his pipe. "Anyways," he continued, "it did a doggoned good job while it lasted. But no more rich crayfish soup. No more fried eel. Back to the dratted codfish full speed ahead." He was amused. He uttered his first laugh since the accident.

It pained us to hear him talk thus of the pot, knowing that his words could very well be the truth—that there was no chance of us seeing the pot again. But it wasn't all pain. Grandpa was talking again and smiling, too. Which was excellent.

We went down to the river, to the pool where the pot had been dunked in the previous evening. The leash was still in the water, trailing downstream. I looked at Milton. He was reluctant to touch the streaming cord and thus make sure. He had a bigger sense of responsibility than I had and was perhaps thinking deeply of what the loss of the pot meant, and he hesitated. So I pulled the leash in, and it came toward me easily. Too easily.

Milton looked at my arms and saw that there was no strain on them. Then he shifted his eye to the water where the cord would break loose. His eyes were almost shut as he looked. The leash finally glided out of the boiling water, unattached, and it was frayed where it had snapped. Milton said nothing. He turned and walked away without saying a word. Poor chap.

I stayed long enough to look downstream, to where the river jigged around a sharp bend; then I untied the cord and wound it small and put it, wet, into my pocket. Who knew? Maybe we would be using it again. Later in the day, when the water had dropped back to near normal level, we would search for the lost pot. We might find it, too.

The rainstorm was a freak at this time of year. We had been caught unawares. I cursed the whims of the weather as I walked away and joined Milton where he was milking Red Gal.

Milking was glum that morning. Milton and I spoke not a word. Milk delivery was better because it had me on the move constantly, and this kept my mind off the lost pot.

The entire village had been taken aback by the flash flood and people were holding lengthy and noisy discussions about it. Down the road there were two landslides within a quarter of a mile of each other. The second, which was the greater of the two, had blocked the road, and four men from the Public Works Department were already busy clearing the pile of mud and dirt. Waiting to go their separate ways as soon as the debris was cleared were a bread van and Riggan's cart. Riggan the butcher was on his cart, holding onto the reins. Of course I didn't have to wait, pedestrians could pass all right; but Timmy that I was, and eager to learn about every screw and bolt that made up a motor vehicle, I began to walk around the van, bending down and peeping under her, touching the lugs and telling myself they were the lugs. I was at this for a considerable time, while the men waited and those who worked away at the slush swapped comments on the flash flood.

"Rain like this is unusual at a time like now," Riggan said. "This is not December weather at all."

"Surprising to me too," the driver of the van said. He was a thin man. He kept an unlit cigar in his mouth as he sat outside on one of the van's fenders.

"It did a lot o' damage," one of the road workers said, leaning on his shovel. "Missa Chaney lose a lot o' bananas."

"I'm worried about the fair," a second worker got in as he took a breath of air. "If this kind o' rain continues next week, the cricket match and the fair will be washed out completely."

Oh my goodness! I thought, realizing that that was true. If the rain fell on Christmas Day as it had fallen that night, there'd be no cricket match and no fair. The cricket grounds would be turned into mud.

No fair! And by then our goodies would have been baked and cooked! What would happen? A total loss on our outlay? Our hopes to get Grandpa a buggy thwarted? I felt upset, and walked away, creating history as I did. It was the first time in my life that I had voluntarily left a motor vehicle.

Back at home I told Milton of the fear of bad weather on Christmas Day. He was calm. To him the rain was just one of those things that happened once in a while. Rain didn't usually fall like that in December, in the dry season. It was unlikely that there would be a repetition next Tuesday. Everything would be all right. There'd be a sunny day, a fair day,

as fair a day as any, and people would turn out in their hundreds. They would come from far and near, from Johnson
Corner, from the hill country, and from James Bay and
farther too.

Milton charmed me with his assurances. He was so calm,
and his words were magical. The way he put it made me feel
better. A whole lot better.

"Let us not panic," he finished.

On that day, which was Thursday, I failed completely in
my task of surprising Trouble in the act of laying her eggs,
or to catch her rising from the hidden nest we guessed she
used.

"Any luck?" Milton asked me in the afternoon.

"Luck in what?" I knew what he meant and was only
stalling.

"In catching up with Trouble."

"I was worried over the fishpot," I said lamely.

"So what's worrying going to do?"

"I was afraid you'd go off looking for it while I was keeping an eye on Trouble. A serious eye I mean."

He pointed at the river, with its torrent still capable of
sweeping us off our feet had we ventured in.

"Are you crazy? Search for a fishpot in that? You want us
to be washed away? And how would we see clearly in that
muddy water, Mister Simpleton?"

That was right. How silly of me, really! I hadn't thought
of the muddiness of the water. Milton was smart; I was the
simpleton all right. Timmy Cassidy, simpleton of the first
order.

"The search for the pot is postponed until tomorrow," he
said, sounding like a general. "And I'll tell you what, Timmy.
We'll come to an agreement. I won't attempt—*attempt*, under-

stand?—to search for the missing pot until after you've done your spying on Trouble tomorrow. Okay?"

"Okay," I said.

So, with this agreement reached on Thursday afternoon, I was all detective on Friday morning after milk delivery.

I spotted Trouble soon enough, not at our place—no sir!— but over at the premises of the Symes's, our neighbors. She was in the act of picking a fight with another pullet when a rooster intervened with a drop of a wing and the go-between agility of a practiced referee and broke up Trouble's intended trouble.

From then on I didn't let that pullet out of my sight.

She wandered from the Symes's place over to ours, only stopping to drink water at the watering can we kept filled near the old fowl coop, in which fowls of normal behavior laid their eggs. Finally she wound up over in Allan Bent's yard. She thereupon began making chortling noises, egg-calling noises. These confirmed my guesses about Trouble. She was laying eggs somewhere.

I kept my eye on her. Then she was going places and I went with her, following, of course, at a discreet distance.

You know what happened? She headed straight for that cluster of pineapple plants and disappeared from view in the tangle. I should have known that if there was a hidden nesting place it would have to be in there. Fowls were no fools even in those days, and, since Onis's rooster had found it a good hiding place, why not another fowl?

There was a tree nearby, a many-limbed and heavy-foliaged mango tree. I hauled myself up into its branches and, with my hands, parted the foliage. I could now see directly down into the clustering pineapple plants and I anxiously awaited Trouble's emergence after laying.

And she wan't in her sanctum sanctorum for more than fifteen minutes either. First came a three-note cackle from her, like an alarm clock going off; then she popped up into view. When she had gone in, she had walked. Now Trouble, lighter by an egg, decided to wing it out. She rose from that thicket in a sudden batter of wings, cack-cacked while in flight, and touched down near the hedge that separated our place from Alan Bent's. Then she burst into a serious cacophony of cackles and, as far as responsibility was concerned, she was through for the day.

Of course, I had seen the exact place she had popped from! Of course, of course! Smack in the center of the thicket that stood like a rocky and ugly island in the unmowed but short grass. Smart bird that Trouble, choosing such a spot. Smart indeed. But not quite smart enough. Or she wouldn't have popped out in flight and betrayed the exact position of her nesting place.

"Little Boy Blue," I whistled as I climbed down from my observation tower.

I guessed it was Trouble's intention to sit on those eggs, hatch chickens, and raise a brood. I wouldn't say that she would have raised decent chickens, but it pleased me that she had started out on the first leg of motherhood. Only she was going to be disappointed, because we needed those eggs as an ingredient for cakes to stock up our stall. Trouble would have to lay herself another clutch of eggs.

Milton was not at home: he had gone to the fields to reap some ground provisions for us to eat over the weekend. So it was up to me to remove the eggs. I did some thinking about how best to set about it. I would get those eggs with a minimum of damage to my hands and legs from the pineapple prickles. In the end I donned a longsleeved shirt and borrowed a pair of Grandpa's old long pants, so long for me that I had to turn up the legs several times. Then a box for the eggs.

There were fifteen eggs in the nest. Fifteen! Spread around in a large nest which Trouble had made of straw. I loaded the box, leaving a single egg in the nest, so that on returning the following day and discovering that the nest had been robbed Trouble would not sustain a completely broken heart. Such

consideration should be spared even a delinquent like Trouble,
I thought. I would have shown my find to Grandpa, but the
old man was snoozing in his armchair, so I set the box down
on a table and shot out to the field to tell Milton.

"Fifteen!"

"That's what I said, Milt. Fifteen beautiful white eggs."

"Golly!" Milton said, showing his teeth. "She gives trouble
but she has her uses. Who would've thought it? Who would
have thought that she could lay that many eggs?"

"I left one in the nest," I said. "I only took fourteen."

"Good," Milton said. "Let's hope that'll make her go on
laying."

"Are you really pleased?" I asked.

"Overjoyed. At this time of year egg prices shoot sky high.
We may have saved ourselves as much as six shillings there."

"Wow!" I said.

"Good work, Timmy," he said.

"Thanks," I said.

He had dug yams, and potatoes as well, and there was a
scraggy-looking bunch of bananas which he had cut from one
of our few trees. He was now looking up at the breadfruit
on a tree, noting the position of a couple of ripe ones. Then
in a zip he was up the tree and two breadfruit whumped to
the ground.

"I'll cook some soup for dinner," he said. That was all right
with me. I loved soup. "I had hoped to catch a couple of good
fish for it, but the river had other plans for our fishpot." He
looked toward the river. It was out of sight, but we could hear
it chortling happily over its bed of stones.

"I think I can spare enough money to buy us some beef
for that soup, though."

That decision made me happy. I would be buying the beef

down at Riggan's slaughterhouse. I was already thinking of the beef Riggan roasted on coals in the slaughterhouse to pass around to early customers.

Milton was gathering the food as if he meant to go homeward, and so I said, "About the fishpot. Aren't we going to search for it?"

"Oh, yes. Though I don't think we'll find it. We don't stand a ghost of a chance."

"We could try," I said.

"Want to go now?"

"Why not?" I said. The fact was that I felt dirty and itchy from having being in the pineapple patch and I could have used a bath.

"All right," Milt said.

We left everything and headed for the river. The water had drained away considerably and was now a transparent blue and very inviting. We stripped on the banks and plunged into the pool where the pot had last been set. We made quite a splash going in and I did a somersault, a specialty with me. The water was cool and tingling fresh and I felt as if I could remain in it forever. But I saw Milton with arms submerged, searching beneath the banks and among the reeds for the missing pot, and I joined him.

We went downstream. I worked with a long pole, poking the deeper stretches of water for the wickerwork pot as we went. We went slowly, and I swam and I dived as I went. We must have been in the water for nearly two hours and covered more than a mile downstream, since we didn't have to waste time searching the shallows, into which we could see at a glance. However, we didn't find the pot. We went as far as the waterfall, and the plunge of water was heavy on our backs and beat the breath out of us. Some way farther down from

the waterfall we abandoned the search. The pot must have
been swept all the way down to the sea, we decided.

We went back upstream, water-soaked, but feeling lighter
now that we had proved beyond doubt that the fishpot had
been swept away, lost forever, and was not merely lying a
little way downstream, waiting for us to pick it up; or for
someone else to do so and keep it for himself.

So that was that. Our protein-provider was lost. Maybe we
would have another made in time, but that would be after
Christmas and the fair.

The fair, the fair—it needed our most urgent consideration.
And after that, Grandpa's rehabilitation.

"What will you call it?"

The countdown to Christmas Day began.

SATURDAY

After milk deliveries and breakfast and doing of the dishes, Milton and I prepared ourselves for possibly the toughest Saturday in our lives. We set off for the woodland about a mile and a half away. Saturday was our usual day for gathering firewood, a week's supply or nearly a week's supply, but on this day we had the responsibility of gathering wood not only for our kitchen fire but also for Mrs. Chaney's oven, in which our goodies for the fair would be baked.

We tramped along the river, going upstream, never out of sight of the clear, clean, idling water which moved slowly across Boswell Flats. The river here didn't seem to want to go any place special and swung this way and that like a snake in motion. We passed tall, clean-trunked bamboos and walked

in the shade of rose-apple trees in scented blossom. Then the
track began to climb.

Jasper Woodland—that was what they called it—was cooler
than out in the open. The trees were thick together, but sun-
light, using the holes in the perforated umbrella of the foliage,
reached the undergrowth below. Beneath the trees the earth
was damp and soft with thousands of rotting leaves, and the
birds screeched and jabbered in the leaves, moving from tree
to tree, a happy band of rovers.

The woodland supplied firewood for the whole neighborhood, and soon there was the sound of scattered hacks and
whacks of cutlasses and axes, drowning completely the bird
song. Other men and boys were at work gathering firewood;
we were not alone.

Milton had a cutlass and I had a small one, too, and we
both concentrated on branches, shearing off the twigs and
cutting them short. We worked without much talking, and
roughly two hours and many palm-blisters later we had collected enough to satisfy our needs. But I did not in those two
long hours devote myself to firewood alone. Not me. Sometimes I took a breather and sat on a stump or ambled off for
a bit, and on one of these occasions I came upon a young parrot struggling to fly. Its wings finally failed and it fell on the
ground near to me, and so it became mine. A pretty thing.

We were ready to start transporting the firewood, but first
we made bundles, lashing the bits of wood with vines. Milton
hoisted a bundle onto his head, and I a smaller one on my head
too. That consignment of firewood was delivered at the
Chaney Great House. The second one as well. We stored
four bundles in the shed which housed the oven, then we returned to Jasper for our own week's supply, and so home.

Back at home I found time to make a small, rough cage

for my parrot out of thin strips of bamboo, and I put a small tin of water in it and fed the bird some peppers. But I could not spend much time with it, not even to give it a name, so it went unnamed for the time being, while Milt and I attempted to give to our premises the Christmassy look.

In Boswell and in other neighborhoods as well, everybody took great care to have their premises looking the dandiest for Christmas. Lawns were barbered, hedges clipped, and flower beds and paths marked out with river stones washed milk-white with a solution of lime. The trees were not neglected. Their foliage was trimmed and their trunks given a whitewash too, so that they stood like massive legs wearing white socks. Everything gleamed for Christmas. Those who could afford it slapped paint onto their houses. Some put new thatching to their roofs, others new zinc. Why shouldn't our premises be in tiptop shape too? Not because Grandpa was disabled!

So Milt and I set to work.

The grass in the front- and backyards had already been cut. Now we turned to moving stones from the riverbed—and what a fine collection of rounded and smooth stones the flash flood had left us! We set up stones around what was left of the flower garden and edged the path leading from the gateway to the front steps. We then mixed the lime with water and daubed the stones a startling white. And not only the stones but the trunks of the trees as well, all four of them: two coconuts, a mango tree, and a spreading guango. Then we took a luncheon break, eating yellow slices of paw-paw fruit and drinking a glass of milk each.

After lunch came house-cleaning. We always scrubbed and polished the floor on Saturdays, anyway. We used a dye boiled from the bark of a tree and wax from the honey comb; our brushes were cut whole from the fibrous sheath surrounding the coconut. I was never keen on floor-cleaning which entailed going on all fours, because my knees always took an awful bruising. But this was Christmas, the season with a different spirit, and I went about the job cheerfully.

We had a few coconuts stored in our cellar but we'd need some more, so Milton shinnied up a coconut tree and pulled some. Not only mature nuts but some young ones as well, three in all: one for me, one for Grandpa, and one for himself. Good old Milt, I thought, as I guzzled my coconut milk.

According to what sun there was above the horizon, night was probably about two hours away. We had time to go down to the river and cut some bamboo which we needed as framework for our stall at the fairground. Milt then ran off to attend to the animals, and when he returned he found that I had a fire going, and supper was prepared in record time.

Then it was night and, though tired and beaten, we legged it to the square to browse around and buy some groceries for the coming weeks.

Sporadic explosions of firecrackers enlivened the village, and the night was full of the noise of boys jabbering and shouting, laughing and screeching. From far away, in the direction of Junction, a hill district to the north, came the high wail of a fife accompanied by the quick-beat of a drum—John Canoe music, according to the beat.

John Canoe dancers were a Christmastime troupe. They masqueraded in costumes and danced to music, traveling from village to village on foot, so that they could dance all the way. Legend has it that their costuming and dancing had begun with a slave called John Canoe, who had been taken from Africa to work on the sugar plantations in the Caribbean. It wasn't all work and misery for the slaves on the plantations: at festive seasons they were allowed to make merry, and John

Canoe was one of their leaders in this merry-making.

So now the tom-tom throbbed away and the fife wailed in the night from the heights of Junction. Maybe they were rehearsing, maybe performing. But one thing was sure: they would be in Boswell on Monday night, Christmas Eve, to perform in the square. I had a date with Boswell square on Christmas Eve!

SUNDAY

We collected nineteen shillings and sixpence from milk sales for the week, an improvement on the previous week and only sixpence short of a pound. Things were looking up.

Sunday school was the same as usual, and Miss Kirby was her old self. But Sunday school didn't last forever, it ended one hour after it started.

Milton had his own penny to plunk into the collection plate and I had mine, so there was no trouble from me in that department. The Chaneys were in church (not Mister Chaney), and Margaret was sitting one pew in front of us when the big service commenced.

She wore a fancy hat with a feather in it and a dress with a skirt that stood out stiff with starch. After church she and Milton talked.

"Well, how is everything coming along?" she asked.

"Fine," Milt said.

"Fine, you say! And Mom's been wondering if you've called off the whole thing. You've brought no money. You haven't brought materials!"

"Oh, that!" said Milt with his usual calm.

"We brought the firewood," I said.

She looked at me as if I were joking.

"That's the least," she said.

"I'll be there this afternoon with some things and money," Milton promised.

"You'd better," Margaret said as a warning. "Have you a stall made?"

"No."

She widened her eyes.

"Why not? And when do you intend to make it?"

"Tomorrow. In the morning, before baking begins."

"You sure like to do things at the last moment." She screwed up her mouth. For some reason or other Milton wasn't looking her straight in the face. He never seemed to look Margaret straight in the face.

"I passed by the fairground this morning," Margaret said, "and the other stalls are up already."

"I know," Milt said.

"So why not yours?"

I took objection to the way she was talking to Milt. She made herself sound too much like a mother—Milt's mother. But I said nothing. I let Milton handle his own problem.

"My reason," Milton began. "Well . . . I want it made at the last moment so that the coconut fronds will be green and fresh. Not wilting, as the others will be."

A good reason to me. Stalls were made out of bamboo, and thatched and walled with coconut fronds. The greener the fronds, the better the stall.

Attaboy, Milton: good reason that.

"Oh," was all Margaret said. She looked around, then went on to new business. "What will you call it?"

"The *stall?*"

"Of course. Aren't you thinking of giving it a name?"

Milton smiled as if something had dawned on him.

"All right," he said, "but I hadn't thought of it."

"Well, you think about it as of now," she said.

"Have you a suggestion, Margaret?" I asked, only because I wanted her to look at me.

"No," she said. "Not yet. Perhaps when the stall *has* been made."

"All right," Milton said. "Let's think about a name for that stall."

Milton then talked to Mrs. Chaney and assured her that the materials he had managed to lay hands on so far, such as eggs and coconuts, and money to buy other things—sugar, spices and the like—would be brought to her that very afternoon.

"Fine," she said. "Very fine." She smiled in a friendly way.

To me she said, "Hello, Timmy! Behaving yourself like a good boy?"

Since Miss Kirby wasn't on hand to contradict me, I said, "Fine, ma'am."

We got a ride home in the Chaneys' car and the chauffeur handled it very beautifully along the road. It was smooth riding all the way and I sat on the edge of the seat with my body forward so that I could see out of the window and count the trees rushing by. I really regretted that the Chaneys didn't attend church more regularly so I could get rides home.

In the afternoon Milton and I set out for the Great House with the eggs and coconuts and money we had saved. It turned out to be a good thing that I had gone along because Mrs. Chaney had left dinner for us. This was wonderful, not merely because it was fricasseed chicken and rice and peas—there was ice cream as well. I loved ice cream.

That night there were more explosions of firecrackers, but no sound of the John Canoe music. Those performers knew better than to rehearse on a Sunday.

MONDAY

First it was helter-skelter for us as we rushed through our morning jobs of milking and delivery. Then it was the stall which next got our attention. Baking wouldn't begin at Mrs. Chaney's until noon approximately, so we had time enough. She wouldn't be starting *our* baking until she was through with hers.

As Margaret had said, other stalls had been constructed already. They stood in a row at the edge of the fairground. A few cricketers were there practicing, too.

Allan Bent was on hand to help us construct the stall. The bamboo for posts and rafters had already been cut, and while Allan dug the post holes, Milton and I gathered coconut fronds for the roof and walls. This meant that Milton had to climb a coconut tree, two trees in fact, and with his cutlass sever the fronds, which came swooshing down to the ground.

Milton was a good provider: possessing foresight, if you get what I mean. He foresaw that ahead of us lay much work in the heat of the sun, which would eventually result in thirsty bodies. So to slake our thirst in the future, he cut a few young coconuts. Later, when the sun got the better of us, we'd cut them open and drink their milk.

I helped drag the fronds to the fairground and, when we got there, we were surprised that Allan had worked so fast. He already had the posts in their holes and we helped him fill the earth in around them and ram it down. He tied the rafters down with vines.

Milton and I roofed the stall while Allan, using some of the fronds, made the walls. This meant standing the fronds' tails up in a line in the ground, and braiding the loose, dangling leaves to give the appearance of a mat.

"Have you found a name as yet?" I asked Milton.

"No," he said. "I have no idea what to call this stall."

"You'd better find a name, though."

"Yes, yes," Milton said. "But I can't think of anything suitable. Why, I've never heard of any stall getting a name before."

"Me neither," I said.

I passed up a frond for him to tie down on the rafters.

"Maybe we'd better call it the Coconut House," I said as a joke.

"Maybe," Milton said. "Come to think of it—that's not a bad name, after all."

Then I saw Margaret coming, and said so. Under her arm she was carrying a box.

"Well?" I said to Milton.

"Well what?"

"Is it going to be the Coconut House?"

"All right, all right," he said. "I'll hear what Margaret has to say to that."

Margaret began smiling even from a distance.

"Hello, hello," she said to Allan and me. Then looking up at Milton perched on the roof, she cocked her head and helloed him but she made it sound like she was saying Hail-lo!

Milton grinned nervously. Everything about him was nervous in Margaret's presence.

"Hi," he said.

"You people are working fast," Margaret said to everybody.

"Yes, Missy," Allan Bent said. "We tryin' our best."

To Milton she said, "So what's it going to be called, Milt?"

Milt she said, just like what I called him sometimes.

"Well," Milton answered. "What about the Coconut House?" he winked at me.

"No," Margaret said and stamped her foot. "No!"

A body would think that she had been bitten by an insect.

"Got a better name?" Milt asked and wiped sweat from his forehead on his sleeve.

"Yes, I have and it's better than that fool Coconut House. It will be called *The Cloud*," Margaret said with more finality than I had thought her capable of. She set down at her feet the box she was carrying.

"*The Cloud!*" I said, appalled. Milton also had a crazy look on his face.

"Yes. And why not?" She looked up. All of us looked up. Even Allan Bent looked up. There was a big swab of cloud floating in the sky.

"A cloud flies high, doesn't it?" Margaret argued. "It stands for hope, then. We must hope for the best in this venture, mustn't we? *The Cloud*," she said. "*The Cloud* it will be."

Nobody said anything.

She bent down now and opened the box and pulled out a large ball of fancy white stuff that looked similar to the clean bank of cloud floating high in the sky.

"What's that?" I asked.

"Artificial snow. We bought it for our Christmas tree. I can spare you this amount to trim the stall. It will be like a cloud, see? Maybe we can hang this in the doorway so it floats. This stall will be called *The Cloud!*"

It didn't make sense for anyone to argue. The stall had been given its name. *The Cloud*. Denoting hope. Hope for success. *The Cloud* indeed.

Milton climbed down from the roof.

"And don't you go ahead and change the name from *The Cloud*," Margaret said, pointing a finger in Milton's face.

"Why should I, Meg?"

Meg, he said. How friendly, I thought.

Margaret tied the ball of white stuff into a cloud bank and hung it over the doorway of the stall. She said that she had a strip of board at home with the words, *The Cloud*, painted on it. She said that could be nailed in place tomorrow morning. She wanted to know where the counter and shelves would be placed, and Milton, using diplomacy to stall the interrogation, cut her one of the young coconuts. She drank delicately like a lady and she was a long time in drinking it, and watching her fooling with it made me double thirsty and I made it known to Milton that I would have mine too.

"We'll soon be finished baking our things up at the house," Margaret said. "You boys haven't much more to do on the stall . . . *The Cloud* I mean. Are you coming back with me?"

"Okay," Milt said. "We'll be along with you." To Allan he said, "You won't be needing us to help with the shelves and the counter, Allan?"

"No, no, Milt. Not at all. I can manage alone."

So we left with Margaret for her house.

We went right into the kitchen after her. In that kitchen there were many fancy things, from the utensils right down to the fireplace, but I wish to say that I didn't pay much attention, because the aroma of Mrs. Chaney's baked things was far too distracting.

Mrs. Chaney had finished her own baking and she was sweating from the heat of the oven. There was a maid in the kitchen too. Mrs. Chaney smiled at us and she said, "Margaret tells me you've done a swell job constructing a stall with Mister Bent's help."

"It's called *The Cloud*," Margaret said proudly. "I named it."

"Now you boys have a lot to do," Mrs. Chaney said. "But first . . ."

She must have noticed me standing with my hands locked behind me, gazing at the mountain of baked goodies, because she proceeded to give us samples of what she had baked. Her samples were good, very good. They made me think she was going to do a wonderful job of baking for us.

Mrs. Chaney immediately set about breaking our eggs into a giant earthenware bowl. She drained each shell of white and yolk carefully into the bowl, and when she had finished treating all the eggs in this way she took up a wooden mixer.

"You do this, Timmy," she said, and shoved the bowl with the mixer toward me.

Following her instructions, I twirled the mixer back and forth and it kicked up quite a storm in the bowl of eggs, beating yolk and white together into a beautiful yellow foam. I twirled away, back and forth—slurp! Oh, this was fun. Slurp-slurp! Baking was fun.

Into another king-sized bowl had gone a mountain of snow-white granulated sugar and bars of butter. With a wooden spoon Margaret was blending these together and, as I watched her, I thought hers was the job of jobs. One's hand had to be gripping the rim of the bowl and it could look as innocent as anything to get a smear of the mixture onto one's hand. After that it would be elementary to get the smeared hand to one's mouth. Unlucky me: to me had fallen the job of egg-mixing. What was there in egg for one to taste? The stuff was foamy and smelt raw.

Poor Milton. His job was even worse than mine. To smash the coconuts open, free the kernels, and then grate them. One funny slip and he could have a finger shredded. I didn't want that job and was glad it hadn't fallen to me.

Now, with all of us going, the inside of the kitchen sounded like a factory with different machines running.

Slurp-slurp . . . slurp-slurp. . . . My sound.

Rub-rub-rub-a-dub-dub. . . . Margaret's sound.

Grrr-grrr-grrr-grrr. . . . Milton's.

Many twirls and slurp-slurps later I finished my job. The eggs had foamed right up to the rim of the bowl and Mrs. Chaney was satisfied. Margaret finished next.

While Milton continued to grate, I watched Mrs. Chaney

and Margaret set to work with rosewater and vanilla and grated nutmeg, raisins and currants too, as if they were a druggist and her assistant.

When the kitchen became too hot a place for me, I took a trip outside and found Freddy, the handyman, clipping the ivy on the wall of the Great House. But I didn't stay with him very long. If he had been washing the car . . . then! And the aroma from the kitchen was luring me back anyway.

Milton had by now finished grating, and I was just in time to see Mrs. Chaney pour a hill of brown sugar onto the fine white shreds to which the coconut kernels had been reduced. This was going to make dozens of coconut cakes, known in and around Boswell as toe-tuhs. Nice-eating cakes they were too, if they were made right, with rosewater and vanilla and nutmeg and raisins; and Mrs. Chaney, it seemed, had these galore.

An hour later Milton was piling firewood into the oven, which was a brick structure about four yards by three and sheltered by a zinc-roofed shed. Freddy left his clipping to give Milton a hand at stoking. Soon the flame was leaping inside and crackling too, and it eventually grew out of the open oven door like a shock of hair. It was so beautiful one had a mind to touch it, but I kept my hand away: I was no fool.

Margaret joined us in the shed. She blew a deep breath of air.

"I'm so tired," she said. "Tonight I'll sleep early and like a log."

"Sleep!" I said. "How could anybody go to bed tonight? Don't you remember this is Christmas Eve? There'll be fun in the square."

"Stupid fun."

"And John Canoe dancers," I said.

"I've seen them so often," she countered.

"You bet you talk this way, Margaret, because you have to go off to bed like any baby."

"I *can* go to the square if I want to," she said positively. "Can't I, Milton?"

"Of course you can," my brother said.

"Me," I said, "I have to go to the square. If I didn't whoop it up tonight, I'd die or the world would end. After all," I concluded, "this night comes only once a year."

"Don't you do too much, you two," Margaret said, meaning Milton and me and making the advice sound as if coming from our mother. "You shouldn't be too tired and sleepy tomorrow. Tomorrow we have a job to do."

I tittered. "In *The Cloud*," I said, and made it sound like a criticism.

"Shut up, Timmy!" she said angrily. "You baboon, monkey, alligator . . ."

I laughed again and Milton looked at me rebukingly. Margaret knew I was criticizing her name for the stall, so she left in a huff for the kitchen.

"Watch your mouth," Milton said. "You irritated Margaret."

"You mean Meg," I said, "don't you?" And he too walked out on me.

Because all the things couldn't have been baked at one time, the oven was lit twice. But we finished the day well, finished producing large trayfuls of light cakes, toe-tuhs, puffs, and sugar buns. Their aroma was bewitching. All those that were burned slightly and ruled by Mrs. Chaney to be unsatisfactory for sale became the property of Milt, me, and Freddy, the handyman. These properties didn't last long in the outside world, however. We stuffed them down.

It was now late afternoon. Electricity had not yet come to Boswell on poles and Mister Chaney was the only man in the village who boasted electricity. He owned a small generating unit and before we left Freddy got it going. It put-putted into life and lights came on in the kitchen.

When we left the Chaney house we left the baked goodies behind. Mrs. Chaney, who had ample storage for them, had offered to keep them for us until fair-time the following day. They were safer with her, anyway.

Night was but a step away and Milton scooted off to the fields to have Buster penned and the other animals attended to, while I was to go on home and have the fire going and get a saucepan on. There wasn't going to be any supper that evening for Milton and me. Only for Grandpa, and that would be in the form of porridge and some of the baked things that I had carried home.

On the veranda I found Grandpa sitting in his armchair. He seemed more alert now than usual and looked up as I came around the corner of the building.

"Well," he said, spitting, "how was it?" He stuck his pipe back into his mouth and he looked amused.

"What, Grandpa?" I asked. "The baking?"

"The foolin', son."

"What fooling, Grandpa?"

"That you two goin' to run a stall and stock it full o' this and that. I'll be doggoned if it comes to anything."

"Watch and see, Grandpa," I challenged. "You watch and see. You'll be sorry by this time tomorrow."

He smiled as much as to say, Poor hopeful. He had not opposed the scheme. He maintained that Milton had been doing a jolly good job in running things around the house, and if he felt now like doing such a fool thing as running a stall at the fair, he was very welcome. He wouldn't do a thing to stop him, but it was a "dratted foolish idee." The fact that Mrs. Chaney and her daughter, plus Allan Bent, were in on it helped give the scheme prestige in Grandpa's eyes, but still he was a bit skeptical. It seemed to please him, though, that he would be having a good laugh at us. He said that our scheme wouldn't come to much. I hoped we would prove him wrong.

Soon it was night and the moon arrived in the sky and there was no true darkness except where shadows fell. The thin wail of the fife lifted high and clear and the quick-beat tom-tom accompanied it. Already the village was banging with firecrackers and after each burst happy voices proclaimed, CHRISMUS! If you mean to shout it good and well there was no other way but to corrupt the word to Chrismus.

Voices were on the road too. They were faint at first, then they grew louder as they came closer, and then they were faint again as they moved away to the square. Everybody was headed for the Boswell square. Everybody. What a night! The John Canoe dancers would be there in time and the rising volume of the fife and tom-tom indicated they were well on their way from Junction.

The big night was here.

We lit the lamp in the hall and gave Grandpa his pipe and Milton cut up and minced his tobacco for him and loaded the pipe and lit it. Grandpa sat in his favorite arm-chair and puffed away as we bade him goodbye.

"Careful now," he said.

"Yes, Grandpa."

"Sorry I can't be there myself."

Cal Symes was on our veranda, waiting for us. His parents had gone on ahead and in the square he would join them. Cal jingled money in his pockets. It sounded like a lot of coins to me.

The square was full and overflowing and more people were pouring in from the hill country and everywhere. Fire-crackers blasted away almost continuously now and the voices shouted the happy word CHRISMUS and the air smelled of the powder of spent crackers. Children scampered along the street, boring in and out among the adults, and some trailed balloons overhead and behind them. Now and again a bal-loon's bursting added to the explosions in the square.

One could get lost in a crowd like this. Milton must have realized that, because he gave me a shilling spending money and, though he did not say so, I understood his action to mean I was on my own.

Since I had a shilling I thought I would do a bit of spending and headed straight for Mister Lethbridge's General Store, the largest of the three business places and the most amply stocked. I wanted my shilling changed into pennies which would jingle, and to buy me a handful of firecrackers and a balloon.

The general store was so crowded that I had to force my way in by using the spaces between the feet of the adults, and nearly got crushed for my efforts. It was a sweating, jabbering, shouting, shifting mass of people, but I reached the counter.

Getting served was another matter.

The store was decorated with brightly-colored paper flowers and bells and fruits. There were decorations hanging from the ceiling and others reaching from wall to wall. The paper from which they were made was shiny and glimmered in the lights of the store. Balloons were also part of the decora-tion: they hung from the ceiling singly and in bunches. They were like oversized fruits in different degrees of ripeness and the wind that entered through the doors and windows and passed over the heads of the people swayed them on their stems.

People shouted their orders and clamored for service, and Mister Lethbridge and his wife, plus two big sons and a couple of hired helpers, were working themselves to death filling orders. Hams passed across the counters. Bottles of rum and wine. Crates of soda water and parcels of rice. Toys. Big parcels, heavy parcels, and light ones as well . . . right down to a tin of curry powder and a packet of black pepper.

A clerk, jolted by my screaming voice, took my order, handing me a penny balloon and a twopenny handful of firecrackers. I specified that the change should be nine copper pennies.

I was about ten minutes getting back to the street through the crowd of customers, but I managed it.

The crowd in the square had multiplied and was as thick as that in the store, but it had more movement in it and wasn't the same hindrance to progress.

Something detonated close to the back of my neck and, turning, I saw it was Cal Symes holding a toy gun to my spine.

"Drop dead!" Cal drawled, but instead I asked him where he'd gotten the gun.

"Bought it," he said.

"What for?" I wanted to know.

"A fourpence and twopence for shots. A twopence buys fifty shots."

That would be a sixpence to get me some artillery and out of ninepence I'd have threepence left. I started back for Mister Lethbridge's store.

I was so long in there that when I returned to the outside world I found the John Canoe dancers were almost there. I was scared of John Canoe dancers. I didn't wish to be caught on street level, so I found a large ackee tree that grew on a bank and overhung the square. I climbed onto a branch from which I could get me a good view of what went on down below.

The drumming came nearer and I soon saw a crowd of people, some holding torches aloft. The dancers were in front and they were cracking whips, and sparks flew from old swords and cutlasses which they clanged together.

The drum moved closer.

Dum! Dum! Dum-dum-dum . . . ! Dum! Dum! Dum-dum-dum . . . !

The whips went C-c-crack! C-c-crack! C-c-crack!

And the fife wailed.

As they danced, the masqueraders were saying words which sounded like, "Oh . . . la-la! Gi' me money! Gi' me money!"

It was for this reason that I feared the dancers. They cornered an individual and danced before him, cracking whips and clanging swords and cutlasses and saying, "Gi' me money." If the individual had the money and the disposition, he would give something which went toward defraying the masqueraders' expenses. If he got scared by the masqueraders and their whip-cracking and spark-making, he might even end up giving all his money. Just dumping the lot in the outstretched hand of the dancer to get himself out of the fix. Some people, so cornered, had even fainted.

Hence my precautionary measure in perching high in the tree.

The huge crowd parted to give them room in the square, and the performers halted to put on their first dance. Some were wearing the heads of horses and donkeys with the massive teeth chopping. Some wore feathers like great dancing birds. Some wore horns like Viking warriors of old. Some carried whips, some swords, some cutlasses, some batons. They were dressed in masks and veils and costumes with frothy frills and outlandish attachments, and all of them were masked.

Dum! Dum! Dum-dum-dum . . . ! Dum! Dum! Dum-dum-dum . . . !

The fife's wail was high and thin with sharp curves of music, and cutlasses clashed in mid-air with swords so that the sparks flew. The dancers stood in one place and shimmied. They jumped high and pranced. Then they began to work the crowd for money.

Oh . . . la-la . . . Gi' me money . . . ! Dum! Dum! Dum-dum-dum . . . Gi' me money! C-c-crack! C-c-crack! Gi' me money . . . !

I was happy to be away from all this in my ackee-tree perch. Other boys had followed me into the tree, and these fools began to laugh at the cavorting of the dancers and so betrayed our position. Soon a trio of dancers were beneath the tree, encircling the trunk and looking up. Which was not all that happened either.

They cracked whips and clanged swords and cutlasses. I had an awfully sick feeling in the stomach and my chest had become a thumping place for my frightened heart. I didn't think the other boys felt too comfortable either, because by now they had stopped their silly laughter. And to make things worse, one dancer thought he would turn the tables on us. Off went his shoes. Up, the frock coat he wore. And up the trunk of the ackee tree he came.

"Now!" the crowd shouted with unkind pleasure.

"Gi' me money! Gi' me money!"

The other boys climbed higher into the tree, but I was out on a branch and remained there as if paralyzed. The masquerader was well up in the tree and my hand automatically went into my pocket, fished out my three remaining pennies, and dropped them into his outstretched hand. Satisfied, he shinnied down the tree again and joined his two colleagues, who had been keeping up a dance round and round the ackee tree, making believe they were hacking it down.

Now I cursed myself. Fool, I said, fool! You should have given only one penny. He would have been satisfied. They were always satisfied.

All was not in vain, however. My encounter with the John Canoe dancer had at least made me face up to my fear once and for all. I was not afraid another minute. Why, I told myself, they were men after all!

I climbed down from the tree and joined the milling crowd. The whips cracked just over my head. Indifferent now, I stood my ground. Sparks flew from swords and I playfully attempted to catch them with my hands. I laughed. This was fun. This was Christmas. This was Christmas in Boswell.

The excitement that flowered with the coming of the John Canoe dancers faded after a time, and I got the opportunity of firing a few rounds of ammunition from my small toy gun.

Pye! Pye! Pye! it went.

Then I thought I'd save some ammunition for later, or for Christmas Day, so I turned to blowing up my balloon.

I ran into Milton.

"Long time no see," I said.

"Timmy, where were you?"

What a question! I thought. "All about," said I. "And you?"

"In the crowd." A pause, then: "Don't you go off again. Stick with me."

"I didn't go off," I said. "*You* went off."

"Then stick with me," he said. "What a crowd!"

"Speaking of sticking," I said. "How about sticking it up?

Real high, Milt!" I pulled my toy gun and terrorized him
with it.

Instead of reaching upward, he asked, "Where'd you get
that?"

"Every Cassidy is a spender," I said. "From the cradle to
the grave. What have *you* there?" In his hand he carried a
small parcel.

"Something."

"I know it's something. But what something?"

"Present."

"For whom?" I persisted.

"Ah!" he said irritably. "Questions, questions."

Of course the John Canoe dancers did not perform continuously. They panted for breath and they needed refresh-
ments, so they punctuated their performance with intermis-
sions, though they didn't remove their costumes or their masks.

Someone in the crowd had a guitar and during the inter-
missions he strummed the instrument for the benefit of the
people who, in their gayest mood of the year, were doing
street dancing. This, however, did not prevent the boys from
exploding firecrackers. I didn't pop any of mine. I would take
them home and pop them early in the morning before it was
quite day, so that Grandpa could hear them. I would bring the
Christmas spirit to Grandpa's ears.

By this time people who had had enough started to go home.
It was about midnight, but the stores were still open and
crowded. On Christmas Eve there was no definite closing time.
Milton and I had no desire to go home at all. It was as if we
hadn't worked our backs sore all day, fixing a stall called *The
Cloud* and baking stuff to put into it. We were enjoying ourselves with all the other boys, making the most of this once-
in-a-year night. Then something happened.

A roll of thunder passed across the sky. Not in an urgent manner or even overhead. Somewhere distant. We saw no lightning, only heard the thunder, but that was enough for Milton.

He looked up into the sky as one who had heard the approach of doom and all he said was, "Let's go, Timmy."

To him the thunder promised rain and that meant destruction as far as the fair was concerned. No fair, no sale for all that baked stuff. All our plans would have been defeated.

I realized now how stupid Margaret's name for the stall was, after all. *The Cloud*. Does a cloud not hold rain? She had perhaps unwittingly invoked rain by naming the stall *The Cloud*. Stupid Cloud, I cursed.

So we went home.

I didn't mind. I had had enough, anyway.

There was light in our house and we found Grandpa up, in the same armchair we had left him in, his pipe still smoking like a steam train.

"Har!" he said as we went in. "Those John Canoes been in the square, eh?"

"Yes," we said, and, "One of them got threepence from me," I announced.

Milton looked surprised at me and Grandpa asked, "A whole threepence?"

So I told my story and Grandpa laughed. There was a light in his eyes that had been absent for weeks and he didn't look so old now to me. Christmas, it seemed, had caught up with him.

"They always work me for money too," he said, "but none ever got more'n a penny at a time from me."

"But I was so scared," I said.

"I understand," Grandpa said. "I understand, son. It's no

easy business to have 'em hold you down an' crackin' 'em whips an' brandishin' 'em swords."

Har! Har! he laughed, and Milton laughed too and I felt so good to see Grandpa laughing again. Christmas had come to him and, to give him more, I pulled my toy gun and fired a shot.

"You're dead, Grandpa," I said.

"Don't tell me you had a gun an' let 'em take your three-pence!" he said. And he har-harred better still.

Then I went outside and exploded a few of my firecrackers. They popped loud and gushed fire and, standing on the ve-randa, I shouted "Chrismus!" each time one exploded.

The sky was almost clean. Clouds were few and none of them was a nimbus cloud. There was no more thunder, either. The moon was riding high and the stars were like sequins fastened on the sky's blue dress. The night was almost like a dark day, only there was no gloom. The light was golden with deep shadows under the trees. The river was a curving ribbon of silver and it was silent now. The thousand arrows of the ubiquitous sugar cane stood erect everywhere: an army of archers with weapons against the sky. Suddenly a cock crowed in the distance, and another took up the alarm, and then another, until all the village cocks joined in this nocturnal watch-keeping.

··{7}··
Presents and Preparations

At about two in the morning we went to bed, but this was no night for sleep. Absolutely not. Not for me, nor for Milton either. We woke up often, and Milton watched the sky for weather developments, and the firecrackers continued to shatter the silence of the night. Nobody, it seemed, slept. I heard people walking and talking on the road, and I thought I might just as well end my pretense of sleeping.

I got out of bed, dressed, and arming myself with firecrackers, let them go in the yard. Milton joined me too, and we let rip. Grandpa soon awoke too and moved around and he was singing a ditty about how he remembered the Christmas morning when Jesus Christ was born.

With our firecrackers expended and with dawn only a step away we decided to go off to the fields to do our milking. Milk delivery would never be so early as on Christmas morning. We still had the moon a few minutes above the horizon, and there was light enough for us to see. Red Gal was up and chewing her cud; maybe the firecrackers exploding in the village were interfering with her sleep.

When we had finished delivering milk and returned to the house, we found Grandpa in high spirits.

"Come, me lads," the old man said. "Let's make some punch."

Everyone, more or less, started Christmas Day with home-made punch, which was not only good drinking but great fun to make.

Grandpa, to me, was back to normal as he hobbled around. He broke the four eggs that Milton had left behind for the purpose, broke them in the earthenware bowl we called a yabba (maybe an Arawak word—I couldn't say for sure), and then he poured in the sugar and Milton mixed the stuff with a spoon. Meanwhile, Grandpa brought a nutmeg out of the cupboard and to me fell the job of grating it.

When Milton was through with mixing the eggs and sugar to a yellow foam, milk was added, good creamy milk from Red Gal's udder, and the nutmeg was dusted in to spice things up. Then Grandpa turned to opening the porter bottle, and herein—the opening of the bottle—lay much of the fun.

Carefully, Grandpa twisted the corkscrew down into the cork and pulled gently. The porter hissed like a sassy girl and Grandpa, using his discretion, administered another pull, a harder one this time. More hissing.

"Stand aside, lads," he advised us and he jerked his hand up and—*voom!*—the bottle became unplugged and for a time I failed to pinpoint what was taking place. Something like a geyser squirted high into the air and soon porter was dripping from the ceiling and, frantically, Grandpa was leaning the bottle into the yabba, saving what he could of the porter.

Grandpa laughed. Not just in his beard but as heartily as he had done on Christmas Eve. He laughed loud and merrily, and he squinted at us, and the porter dripped from his beard like globules blooming out of moss. It was like old times, just like old times.

Grandpa then added milk from a young coconut and mixed it around in the now darkened foamy stuff, and the punch was ready. It was still foaming and it looked good and rich and it was sweet and silky to the taste.

I drank half of my glass and stopped for breath, and Grandpa said, "Drink up, lads. Drink up." So Milton and I finished our glasses and had them refilled. Grandpa then drank a tall glass full and his Adam's apple made quick excursions back and forth in his throat. Then he was finished and he burped a couple of times.

Grandpa already had a mustache, a genuine one, but Milton and I also got mustaches now from the foam of the punch. For this reason I spent the next couple of minutes in front of the mirror, having a preview of myself as a man wearing a mustache. I thought I was going to look good.

Yes, this was Christmas.

"Chrismus!" I shouted as I ran out onto the veranda. "CHRISMUS!"

Soon Allan Bent came over to our yard. As he walked he whetted a long butcher knife with a file and, by the way he was licking his lips, I thought he, too, had had his Christmas-morning punch. Grandpa was on the veranda, leaning over the rails and he was smiling, all over his face, and he said, "Merry Christmas, Allan."

"Same to you," Allan greeted him. "And a prosperous New Year too."

Milton and I wasted no time. We began to round up the

young goat which Allan had come to slaughter for us. Allan
was quite professional at the job too, although, butchering for
him was a once-in-a-year occurrence. When he had finished
dressing the meat, he weighed it. Milton hopped around the
yard merrily when he learned the weight. Eighteen and a
quarter pounds of meat! A lot of meat for the curry pot, and
a lot of curried goat for the fairgoers, who would be paying a
shilling a plate for the stuff. We were going to make money.
There were great possibilities in this venture.

"Good meat, eh, Allan?" Grandpa said. "You take a couple
pounds o' that meat an' boil it into a soup an' you'd go hoppin'
mad for soup every livelong day."

We all laughed.

Squawk! went my baby parrot in its cage. I had named it
Bingo. I would have to teach Bingo to make more appropriate
comments than that. But Bingo's squawk reminded me to feed
it some peppers. *Squawk!* it said, and gobbled them up.

Mrs. Bent soon came through the gap in the hedge which
the Bents and ourselves used in exchanging visits, and she was
carrying a cardboard box.

"Merry Christmas, Mista Cassidy."

"The same to you, Ethel."

"Merry Christmas, Milton an' Timmy."

"Merry Christmas, Mrs. Bent."

In the box she was carrying three bottles of pop and a new
pipe for Grandpa and a balloon for me and a comb for Milton.
We exclaimed over the presents and, before Mrs. Bent could
cross through the hedge again, Grandpa said, "Wait there,
Ethel." He swung himself off the veranda and out into the
yard. Taking the butcher's knife from Allan, he divided the
goat's liver and the heart into two equal parts, and each portion
got a kidney. Then he cut a piece of shoulder off and dropped

it onto one portion. He lifted this portion with his calloused hand and put it into Mrs. Bent's cardboard box.

"Here, Ethel," he said. "Christmas is a time o' giving, eh?" Mrs. Bent laughed a hearty Christmas laugh, showing all her teeth.

"Thanks, Mista Cassidy," she said. "Thanks a lot." She turned to Allan. "We'll have a wonderful dinner from this, won't we, Allan?"

"Yes, dear," Allan said.

It sounded a bit strange to me, hearing Allan use the word "dear." It seemed he wasn't the kind of man who had such a word in his vocabulary. But then maybe he used it because it was Christmas.

Still merry-faced, Mrs. Bent went back through the hedge to her yard.

The other portion of meat which Grandpa had divided was ours, of course, plus the head and four feet. They made a sizeable dinner for three people considering that two of them were children, but this was Christmas, a time of plenty.

Then began the cutting and chopping up and the seasoning of the meat destined for the curry pot. Allan was cook. We had nothing to worry about. Good old Allan would do everything. Allan Bent—amateur butcher and professional cook of curried goat. Hip-hip-hooray!

Quite unexpectedly, Margaret came into our yard. She was carrying something held in her hands behind her and, of course, I wanted to see, so I dashed out to meet her. But each time I attempted to spy on whatever it was, she spun out of my way.

"Oh, you busybody!" she said finally, and handed the parcel to Milton.

It was one of the prettiest parcels I had ever seen, done up in Christmas paper, and tied with a blue ribbon.

"For me?" Milton asked.

"Yes. And Timmy too."

How could my brother, Milton, be so dumb! For whom else but us indeed?

"Open it," I said.

Milton gave me an ugly look that was supposed to have silenced me, but I said, "I want to see it. There is something in it for me, isn't there? I have my rights."

"Wait!" he snapped.

"And waiting kills," I grumbled.

Margaret moved off to greet Grandpa first and then Allan, who was busy seasoning the meat. Milton went into the house, taking the parcel unopened with him. Why, the stubborn, stupid . . . ! But he was returning now and—golly!—he was carrying a parcel of his own. The wrapping wasn't very handsome but this surprise parcel was enough to still my fury, because I badly wished to know what it contained. It didn't look like the same one I had seen him with in the square on Christmas Eve. For one thing this was bigger.

Smiling, he handed it to Margaret, and then it was the same thing all over again. Those teenagers!

"For me?"

"Yes," he said. Only there was no Timmy who had a share in this.

Meanwhile I was grumbling for my present, which was bowtied within a box with Milton's. If he could bear the suspense of waiting to know what was in it, I couldn't. So I continued to apply pressure and eventually he yielded, untying the ribbon. He handed me a mouth organ almost a foot in length with silvered sides. It was a handsome instrument. I jumped in the air and shouted hooray and thanked Margaret and shook her hands, saying: "Wonderful, wonderful!" And in an instant I was an organist.

Milton's gift, however, jerked me to a standstill. It was a fancy penknife, and frankly, it was the fanciest knife I had ever seen. It was equipped with two cutting blades, a large and a small, a bottle opener, a corkscrew, and a pair of tiny scissors. It also had a chain attached to it with which Milton could connect it to his trouser belt.

The moment Milton yielded to my demands to open our parcel, Margaret succumbed to her curiosity and untied and unwrapped hers. Wow! There they were—two gifts together. One was the parcel I had seen Milton with in the square, and the other was a box made from the best of cedar-boards, shining with varnish and smelling of it. Margaret looked at Milton, her eyes smiling; then she slipped the catch and opened the box. Inside was carpeted with green felt and there were four compartments—three small ones in a row to the back and a large one in front.

"Guess what that is," Milt challenged.

"A jewel box!" Margaret answered proudly.

"Right the first time," Milt said, outdoing her with proudness. "And I made it too."

Now I knew why he had spent so much time at the workshop of Mister Romney, the carpenter.

"It was a bit difficult," he said, "but I managed."

"I love it," she said.

"You do?"

"Yes. It's so nice, really."

"I wondered at first if you would like it."

"Don't be ridiculous. It's charming." It was nice hearing her use the word "ridiculous." She got all the letters to work.

They laughed.

"What's in this other?" Margaret asked, holding up the
second gift.

"Open it," he said. "You won't get bitten."

So she opened it, her fingers delicate and slow. This turned
out to be a set of three handkerchiefs, folded in triangles.

"Ooooh!" she said. "Ooooh!"

I felt like a pauper. Everybody had given me something and
I had given nothing. Then I had an idea.

"I have a present for you too, Margaret," I said. I wouldn't allow Milton to outdo me that much. Two gifts and I had given none!

"A present?" Margaret asked. "That's nice."

Both she and Milton exchanged glances as if they thought I was joking.

"Don't you believe me?" I asked Margaret.

"Sure, Timmy," she said. "But where is it? The present?"

"It's a parrot," I said.

Squawk! the bird said.

Margaret looked now and saw the small green fluff of feathers. Obviously she hadn't noticed the bird before.

"Oh!" she said, pulling her shoulders up. "That's dandy. Isn't it sweet?"

"What a cage!" Milt said, meaning it was too roughly made. "I'll have to make a new one for you, Margaret."

"That's sweet of both of you," Margaret said. "I'll take it when the new cage's made. What's his name?"

"How do you know it's a he?" I challenged.

Margaret laughed. "All right, bright boy. What's *its* name?"

"Bingo," I said.

"That's a pretty name," Margaret said.

I felt satisfied. I had done what I could. Grandpa, watching us standing in the yard near the veranda, seemed satisfied too. He was smiling.

But this was not the end. Freddy now entered our yard with gifts from the elder Chaneys. Two shirts for Grandpa and a necktie too, and for Milton and me a pair of shoes each. Brand new shoes, shining as mirrors and nice in style.

I blew some wild music on my mouth organ until Margaret suggested we go to the fairground and put the finishing touches to the stall—*The Cloud*, pardon me. And so we sauntered down there.

The other stalls didn't look so good to me. The palm leaves on them had begun to wilt badly. *The Cloud*, however, was clean and fresh and was different from the rest—designed differently, almost round as a Zulu hut, whereas the others were mere lean-to's.

Some men of the Boswell Eleven were on the green practicing for the cricket match. One man was bowling the ball at another, who batted in front of a single stump. A semicircle of six fielders were picking the ball up each time the batsman hit it.

We put the finishing touches to *The Cloud*, Margaret supervising, and soon we had that round stall all trimmed up with wild flowers plucked near at hand. The ball of artificial snow which represented a cloud bank was still hanging in the doorway as we had left it the previous day. Then Margaret remembered the painted sign she had up at her house and she sent me to fetch it. When I returned with it, Milton climbed up and tied it onto the front of the stall. The letters grinned in glimmering paint. *The Cloud*, they said.

According to Margaret's watch, it was getting close to tenthirty, and it was a relief for Milton and me when Margaret decided that everything on the stall was done and announced that we could leave. She went home, and we went to our house.

Allan had made a fire in our yard and it was bright and crackling under the pot, and the curried goat, nearly cooked now, already had a tantalizing smell.

Milton lit the kitchen fire and hurriedly began to prepare our own Christmas dinner, of goat's meat and rice. While he cooked, I thought that I would find me a job to do, so I cleaned up my cart the best I could. I was going to have work for it, come time for the fair. I would have liked to slap some paint on it, but there was none and, moreover, it was too late for that now. But I had chalk and I thought that chalk would do just as well. White chalk and red. I was imaginative. I would show them.

I chalked the whole works white and then, using the red chalk, I wrote in letters all around the cart, on all four sides: *The Cloud. The Cloud. The Cloud. The Cloud.*

Margaret would be proud, and Milton pleased that she was proud.

·{8}·
Two Clouds
and a Grand Total

We had put in quite a bit of work for the fair already, and there was yet so much that lay ahead. For instance, there was the transfer of the baked goods from the Chaney Great House to the fairgrounds. We made four trips in all, taking all the baked goods in cartons.

Allan had had no less a zeal than us in this project. He had suggested that we include shaved ice and syrup—snowball to us —on our list of fare; and when Milton had pointed out to him that we were short of funds, Allan had put up the money on the understanding that, after the sale, he would be repaid. So Allan had managed this part of the project, had boiled the syrup himself and colored it red and bottled it too. He knew that snowball was a favorite with children, as it gave them a chance of exhibiting their tongues left red by the syrup. Allan had gone further: he had ordered the ice, a large block that came from James Bay by truck, in a sack wadded with sawdust. He carried the big block of ice to the fairgrounds for us, and Milton and I took the bottles of syrup on our fifth trip.

This was going to be a day, I thought. People were gathering fast. Two men at the gate were collecting money. They hadn't charged us any admission fee as yet, except the half crown payable by all stall owners, since we were not dressed up for the fair.

The visiting cricketers were coming. You could hear them from a mile away, in the same way we had heard the musicians a long way off. They, too, traveled in a truck and they were making music as the musicians had done. The musicians had made instrumental music; now the cricketers made singing music.

I wanted to see them arrive—the cricketers. I stood my ground. Soon the truck in which they traveled came into view, and the cricketers and also the men and women who accompanied them were standing, waving handkerchiefs and hands over the rails of the open truck. And they were singing:

> *Boswell sent an' called us!*
> *And we must go!*
> *Boswell sent an' called us*
> *And we must goooo!*

As the truck pulled in at the entrance to the fairgrounds, everybody in it, men and women alike, gave a lusty Hip! Hip! Hoooray! Hip! Hip! Hoooray! It sounded as if a hundred people had shouted into a loudspeaker.

I was so excited that I ran all the way home, only to find that Milton had already taken a bath in the river and was returning. I had to have my bath in the river too. In those days a boy ran a grave risk by bathing at home in a tub: if he were

caught doing it, the news would spread that there was a new
sissy in Boswell and such a boy would rapidly lose face. Even
though I would have liked to save time by bathing at home, I
didn't think it was a safe risk.

I grabbed my towel off the rack, took the soap out of Milton's hand while I was still in the act of running, and was on
the riverbank by the time anyone could have said Jack Robin-
son. I shed my clothes in brutal haste, tearing at them, until I
was rid of them. Then, with my hands clasped out in front of
me, a pint-sized Tarzan, I dived in.

Bathing in the river sometimes ran into two hours for us
boys, but this was no time for swimming round and round,
for climbing into the tree—our springboard—for a dive, or for
somersaulting in the water and floating on the back when we
got tired. This was a time only for a dive, followed by a quick
soaping and another dive to wash the soap off. And then out.

Drying.

Into clothes.

And uphill to the house at a run.

Milton and I wore our new shoes. Mine burned me at first,
but I would be all right. We both wore new pants bought for
the fair, and identical shirts of cotton, decorated with beach
scenes and others from Jamaican life.

Champion was hopping mad to follow us, but we had to
leave the poor fellow behind. A fair was no place for a dog
like Champ. Grandpa wished us all the best and he said goodbye to us from the veranda and waved his pipe at us when we
were at the foot of the hill.

There was a large shifting crowd on the fairgrounds and
more people were streaming through the gate. The music was
playing now.

Allan had a job as umpire in the match and was unable to

help us in the selling of our goods, but we had everything so well organized that we would manage without him. Margaret and Milton would be in the stall, Margaret handling the baked stuff and Milton the curried goat. I would sell the snowball.

Now this was where my handcart came in handy. Already equipped with bottleholders, the cart was just right for carrying syrup bottles, and I calculated that I would do brisker business if I took the snowball to the people rather than allowing them to come to it. One small disadvantage, however: the cart could only hold a twenty-pound block of ice at a time. But that was easily overcome. I could chip a block of the right size from the larger mother block, go forth and sell to the people, and return to *The Cloud*, the depot center, for more.

So while Milton and Margaret sold inside the stall, I would work outside. And what a place to work! I was with the people, could see everything that went on, watch cricket even, listen to the music, and mingle with the dancers. All this I could do, and still perform my job.

When Margaret saw the way I had prettied up my handcart with chalk and named it *The Cloud* in imitation of the stall, her eyes sparkled, and she smiled at me and gave me a wink, and I knew that she was completely reconciled with me and probably loved me too. I began to load up *The Cloud* that was on wheels, but couldn't help sparing a few glances at what went on around me.

The fair, it seemed, was going to make history. To all appearances it would grow into a whopper. People were streaming through the gate almost continuously; gay, laughing people; men and women, boys and girls. Some marched straight to the bandstand, some to the rim of the cricket oval, which was smack in the center of the field, while others browsed around the stalls, buying goodies already.

Being different from the others in every way and in the charge of two young people, *The Cloud* was a winner from the very start. From far off people spotted the big white ball swinging over the door of the stall and they came up to see what it was and what it meant. Once there, they began to patronize the stall.

"One curried goat!"

"A toe-tuh, please!"

"May I have a couple o' sugar buns, Miss Chaney?"

"Two more goat dinners, Milton, with plenty o' curry on them! And hurry!"

The boys and girls of Boswell wanted to know, and very badly at that, what Margaret and Milton were up to. Obviously, the boys were jealous of Milton; the girls were frankly popping with curiosity. I, they thought, had the answers and so they started a barrage of questions.

"What are they doing in that stall?"

"Selling," I said. "Can't you see?" Heh-heh!

"But whose stall is it?"

"Ours."

"Ours, who?"

"Why, Milton's and mine!"

"*Milton's and yours!*"

"That's what I said, sonny boys." As casual as I ever could be.

A breather, then: "So what's she doing in there?"

"Do you mean Margaret?"

"Yes. She."

"Oh. She's helping us you know," I said, putting the bottles of syrup into the cart and whistling as if I hadn't even an audience.

"The whole thing is a lie," somebody said.

"All right. It's a lie then." Phew-phew-phew . . . More whistling. Let them sweat. And I turned away to get my small block of ice chipped, but the questions started coming again.

"Are you telling the truth, Timmy?"

"Of course I am."

"Cross your heart."

I crossed it.

"Where'd you get the idea?"

"It wasn't mine you know."

"Whose then?"

"Milton's and Margaret's."

"How come she's in it?"

"She's a friend of ours. Didn't you know?"

"And the money—what will you and Milton do with all the money you'll make, Timmy? Spend it?"

"Spend it we shall, but not foolishly, friends."

When all this had soaked in, they wanted to know where we had gotten the money for this big venture.

"Oh, that! We saved. We sold milk and saved the money. We got the eggs and coconuts and things like that without buying them, and the goat—it was Milton's. What other money we needed—and that wasn't much—we borrowed." I made it a terse explanation.

They looked again at *The Cloud*, looked with awe, then jostled one another for a peep inside it at my brother and Margaret, and a lot of them who had had pockets full of money on Christmas Eve weren't feeling too happy now. They were thinking of themselves as real fools not to have lit upon a money-making venture like ours.

But I had my job to do and couldn't afford to lend them my shoulder to cry on. Taking a last look inside *The Cloud*, I saw Milton ladling out savory curried goat into a plate and

Margaret standing behind two Himalayas of baked goodies covered with white towels. Snow-covered mountains of goodies. She saw me and squinted at me and, turning, I grabbed my loaded handcart, *The Cloud* that moved.

"Bee-beep!" I said as if I were a car horn. "Bee-beep!" I shoved off into the crowd and some of them followed me.

"Snowbaaaall!" I shrieked. "Beat the heat! Use a glass of snowball!"

I pushed my cart in and out among the shifting people, bee-beeping all the while, but I didn't get far before they started to buy.

"A glass here, Timmy!"

"I'll have one too."

Quickly I shaved the ice off the face of the twenty-pound block I carried in the cart, emptied the full shear into the glass, and poured the rich red syrup on top. Ravenously, the ice soaked up the syrup, and I added a little water to dilute the syrup and also as encouragement to the ice to melt faster. I had a small bucket of water in the cart too, so that I could wash the used glasses right on the spot. I had thought of everything, I had.

The sun was high in the sky now and was uncomfortably fierce for a December sun, but this was what I wanted. It suited my kind of business. The heat made the people languish for something cool and I had the stuff for them. Of course, I wasn't the only vendor of snowball. There was a man from Johnson Corner with snowball too, but he had come to the fair with a massive cart that was cumbersome to move about in the crowd. So he was forced to stay put in one place. Another man, this one from Boswell, was selling ice cream, but he, also, was staying put in his stall and, if he had ever had the thought of working the crowd, I would have had the advantage. A cone of ice cream sold for a threepence, my glass of snowball could be had for half that price.

"Snowbaaall!" I shrieked and moved on.

Then: *Pow!*

"Wow!" from the crowd, especially from those people who lined the cricket oval. "Six runs!" they said.

"What a straight drive!" somebody commented. "You saw that?"

That was the cricket match already under way.

But cricket's excitement is never sustained. Sooner or later there had to be a lull and—here it was now! So the people were again pressing me for snowball. My right hand was going all the time, shaving ice and pouring syrup. There was a line of eight or nine waiting to be served.

Not enough glasses, I lamented. I'm short of glasses and hands.

But deliverance came in the person of Cal Symes, my neighbor and buddy.

"Want help, Timmy? I could wash the glasses for you."

Good-natured Cal.

"All right, Cal," I said. "You wash them while I serve."

We were a team. I shaved the ice, poured the syrup, and collected the penny half penny for each sale, and Cal washed the glasses. And when the water in the bucket was becoming dirty, Cal threw that away and ran off to the standpipe to re-fill the bucket with clean water.

Soon we had a bunch of red-tongued children behind us, following us wherever we went.

"Snowball!" I shouted. "Snowbaaall!"

I must have put real force into my voice because I saw Allan Bent look around at me. He was wearing the white coat that umpires wear. He waved to me and I waved back. His wave asked a question: *How are you doing, Timmy?* Mine answered that question: *Smashing, Allan. Just smashing!*

I soon sold out what ice I had brought along and I steered back toward *The Cloud* for more. When I passed by the unwieldy cart of the man who stood in one place and sold his snowball, he gave me a dark look as if he thought me an insect that had attacked his choice tomatoes or other vegetables. That amused me. I could guess at his feelings. Poor chap. He didn't stand a chance while I roamed the field, and he knew it.

Inside our stall was crammed full of people. It reminded me of Mister Lethbridge's General Store on Christmas Eve. The people were pushing and shouting for service with about the same amount of enthusiasm.

The mountains of goodies had been reduced to hills, and erosion by Margaret's busy hands was fast reducing them to mounds. I was happy. Milton was sweating at his work, too, and some people who couldn't get inside the stall were tearing at the walls, making breaches in the flimsy coconut fronds, and were bribing Milton with fancy words to pass them plates of rice and curried goat. He served them, too, and collected the money—everything done through the holes the customers had made in the wall. Oh, goody!

Content with what I saw, I set aside the empty syrup bottles I had used and took some fresh ones. I also topped up another bottle I had begun to use. Then the ice. I chipped me another block and Cal, who was still working with me, had all the glasses as clean as a whistle and the bucket refilled with clean water.

I pushed out into the crowd to sell my second consignment of snowball.

"Bee-beep!" I said as I maneuvered through the crowd. "Bee-beep!"

When the orchestra was not playing, the local musicians with fifes and drums gathered near the maypole. Boys and girls, wearing the greatest assortment of Christmas hats a body ever saw, were doing the maypole dance. Round and round. In and out. Wrap under, strap over. Round and . . . I steered away. I had my sales to make.

When I finally returned to *The Cloud* I found Mrs. Chaney there, probably come to see how Margaret was getting on. She was all smiles, and her presence, it seemed, was attracting more people to our stall.

Mister Lethbridge of the general store was there too, and he was talking with her. Mrs. Chaney must have broken the news of our venture into business to him, because he looked my way and gave me such a smile that would have made a blind boy blush. Miss Pinkerton, the postmistress was also there. Clutching her handbag tightly under her arm, she greeted both Mister Lethbridge and Mrs. Chaney. Mister Chaney, who must have stopped somewhere in the crowd, came up now. He looked much older than his wife and was wiry, whereas she was plump. Both of them had fair skins, but he was the darker of the two.

The Friendship Eleven had been put to bat first and, although their scoring had started off impressively, they did not live up to it. With the score at a paltry forty-two, they were dismissed.

The interlude which followed now, during which the Boswell men prepared themselves for bat, proved helpful for sales. All those ardent cricket fans who hitherto had found it impossible to take their eyes off the ball, now flocked to the stalls for food and drink. If I had had enough glasses I could have sold so much snowball that I probably would have dropped dead working at it.

Allan Bent sought me out. The snowball department of the venture was his baby. He wanted to know how I was doing.

"Fine," I chirped. "Can't you see?"

He stood there and grinned for a second or two, exhibiting his tobacco-stained teeth.

"Who would believe it?" he asked. "Who?"

Then he took the ice-shear from me and made a few brisk sales.

"If I had more glasses, Allan," I said. "If only I had more glasses. I could sell twice as much."

"You're right," he said. "We could do with more glasses. How's the syrup?" he asked a group of boys who hung around.

"Oh," they said. "Sweet and red, Mister Bent." And they lolled their tongues to show how red the syrup was.

Allan was pleased. He left me then to look in on Margaret and Milton in *The Cloud*.

Making good use of the interlude also, the musicians were belting out some hot numbers, so hot that many people danced on the spot in front of the stalls, danced with heaped plates of curried goat in the hands, or cakes or pop bottles or glasses of snowball to their mouths. But others ran pell-mell over to the bandstand and danced there.

"Snowbaaall!" I shrieked, anxious for sales. "Beat the heat the snowball way! *Snowbaaall!*"

The cricket match resumed and the opening batsmen of the Boswell Eleven began to knock the ball all over the place. Seeing this and predicting a victory, the crowd could not contain their excitement, as the batsmen cover-drove, straight-drove, and slammed away.

"Six runs!"

"A four!"

"Hip!" they said.

"Hip!" they said.

"Hooray!"

As I saw it, if the Boswell boys continued batting in the glorious manner they were doing, it would be a matter of minutes before they would run up the score of forty-two and hit the deciding single, or four, or six runs to finish the match. I circled back to *The Cloud*. I would be prepared for the big spending that would follow a victory—if victory was to be the Boswell Eleven's.

Milton and Margaret were sharing the space in the doorway of the stall and, like everybody else, were watching the cricket. Good for them. But I had work to do. I was going to set up shop permanently outside our stall. Now I would let the people come and get their snowball. And they would come too. Soon there would be no cricket for them to watch. I bared the face of what remained of the mother block of ice and washed it clean of sawdust. Milton gave a hand in washing all the glasses and I set up the syrup bottles on a table. Now I was ready for the big spending.

At last the Boswell boys won the match for the loss of only one wicket. Then the music sounded, and I can never remember a gayer moment than that in Boswell. Suddenly the people were everywhere, and stall owners who had stood idle to watch the match, now scampered back for the big sale.

Me? I was ready. Me? I shaved ice until my poor arm hurt. Then Milton was by my side and helping me.

"The curried goat is all finished," he said.

"What?"

"Yes," he said. "Give the ice-shear here."

I gave it to him. He did the shearing and the syruping while I played the role of cashier. I was very happy indeed. We were in on the money.

A block of ice weighing four hundred pounds, as ours weighed, was a lot of ice, and in those days cost only two shillings. Using the shear on it was really akin to smoothing wood with a plane. You took only a thin part off at a time and you rammed it into a glass and poured the syrup on. At ordinary times this fetched a penny, but on occasions such as a fair, when people were free-handed and, most of all hot, a half-penny was added.

We soon discovered that our syrup was running out, and Milton began to be less generous with it; but with all his pinching the syrup did not last. We were soon sold out. A big slab of ice remained and we pricked it into bits and handed them out.

I deposited all the snowball money with Milton, who put it separately from the curried goat money, and then I browsed around, looking in at the dinner party by now under way for the cricketers and umpires. Catching Allan Bent's eyes, I used my arms in a wave from side to side to give the signal that the snowball had been sold out. He looked pleased, very pleased, and nodded to me; and then the Boswell captain rose to speak and I moved on.

The crack of a gun forced me to steer for the shooting range. There I saw several men waiting their turn to have a go at the bull's-eye, but aiming the gun now was Riggan the butcher. He was stretched out on the turf, his elbows on the ground. He steadied the gun, sighted along the barrel and fired. The echo of the gun's report slammed against the distant hills and rolled back while somebody ran down to the bull's-eye to have a look. The way he moved his arm meant the shot had gone wide.

Serve Riggan right, I thought. What did he want with the

giant ham they were shooting for anyway? He was already surrounded with so much meat.

I left the shooting area. I was such a busy boy.

I reckoned that if we had had twice the baked foods and curried goat and snowball, we would have sold them all in the spending that mushroomed after the victory of the Boswell Eleven over the Friendship men. The people soon reduced Margaret's pile of cakes and toe-tuhs and puffs and sugar buns to nothing, and now we were all free to participate in the merry-making—that is, after a lengthy counting of money and figuring out of profits. Allan Bent and Mrs. Chaney, our patrons, were there of course and the figures were:

Margaret: Nine pounds thirteen shillings and sixpence.
Milton: Five pounds nineteen shillings.
Timmy: Two pounds one shilling and fourpence half-penny.
Grand total: Seventeen pounds thirteen shillings and ten pence half-penny. (Almost fifty dollars.)

Subtracting an expenditure of three pounds fifteen shillings, including one pound borrowed from Mrs. Chaney and ten shillings from Allan, that left us with a clear profit of thirteen pounds eighteen shillings and tenpence half-penny. Of course, if Milton were to count in the price of the kid, valued at thirty shillings, that would have reduced the profit; but he had decided that the kid was part of his contribution.

Milton would have padded off to acquaint Grandpa of our overwhelming success; but he didn't get far. We saw Grandpa swinging on his crutches, coming through the crowd.

"I couldn't stand it no longer," he said. "It was goin' to burst me open, the waitin'. I had to know."

He greeted Mrs. Chaney and Mister Chaney and everybody

else with a "Merry Christmas and a prosperous New Year" and they all wished him the same and shook his calloused hand. He thanked Mrs. Chaney for her gifts and her help and large heart and, when he learned of our success, this is how he began his address to the gathering:

"There's no Cassidy known to me that can't make good. These boys o' mine I tell you, they's headed for great things. They's great boys and nothin' is ever goin' to stop 'em . . ."

Then he saw Margaret.

"Missis Chaney," he said to Mrs. Chaney, "you've got one o' the loveliest an' finest daughters. I tell you this younger generation . . . What'd we do without 'em? These three angels decide to run a stall . . ."

I looked at Margaret. She worked her mouth so that it silently said, *The Cloud*, and then she winked at me.

Grandpa made a bow to Margaret and he went on talking and he nearly made this the best part of the fair.

But he was not wrong either. Margaret had done so much to make the venture a success. Without her perhaps it would have failed.

I had some spending money that had been given to me by Milton and I patronized some of the stalls. Mark you, I was not hungry, and most of what I purchased found its way into the mouths of the boys who had followed me around when I was selling snowball: Cal Symes, Josh Tingling, Onis, and others. Funny: only a night ago they were the millionaires, but now they were eating out of the hands of one who was a pauper at the time.

I did some dancing. Success in our venture had gone not only to my head and put me in a perpetual laughing mood, but it had trickled down into my legs as well, and I did some pretty good dancing (judging from the crowd I drew) with

Nancy Lettman. I was no exhibitionist, but then, on a day like that, who was a shy boy? Nancy Lettmann was one of those fancy dressers that made a fairground sparkle and, without doubt, could dance. So it became a question of who would out-dance whom. I don't think I was out-danced. If anything, both of us tied in the contest. But I danced and danced until the sun dropped behind the hill and the shadows crept in. And even when the fair ended at seven o'clock, I was still dancing.

··{9}··
Pal Joe

Now events began to move quickly. On the day after Boxing Day we went to see Mister Vincent, the wheelwright at
Johnson Corner, about the buggy for Grandpa. We were that
anxious. We would have gone on Boxing Day, mark you, but
we allowed for the fact that Mister Vincent could still be on
holiday and not even at home. But we found him when we
went. Allan Bent went with us and he, of course, did the
talking.

As I understood the story, Mister Vincent was once a man
with the traveling itch and had used a buggy; but now that
he was old, he had put the vehicle away and was staying at
home. The old buggy was in the large workshop. One wheel
was off and it was minus the shafts and the canvas top needed
patching or replacing—I didn't know which. But otherwise
the buggy was in good shape. Even the gong to be operated
by foot was working. In the workshop too, were the begin-

nings of a new cart that Mister Vincent was hard at building.

"You mean you're not joking about wanting to buy that old buggy?" he said to Allan and wiped sweat from his face.

"No jokes, Mister Vincent. What you askin' for it?"

"I didn't figger on selling," Mister Vincent said. Then he took a good look at Allan and, smiling, he said: "I didn't figger you'd want to buy a buggy, Allan. You getting rich or something? Or the bones getting weary?"

Allan laughed.

Mister Vincent was oldish; bent at the shoulders. His spectacles were steel-rimmed and his mustache like handlebars. He was wearing working overalls and his hands were dirty. In one he held a hammer. He laughed at Allan and showed his yellowing teeth.

"You won some money, Allan?"

So Allan told our story and at the end of it all, Mister Vincent removed his cap and scratched his gray hair.

"I dunno," he said, looking at the buggy and then at us. "It needs fixing."

"But you will sell?" Allan asked.

"Yes, yes. Of course I'll sell. I'll *have* to. This here reason you gave me, Allan . . . How could I not?" And again he looked at us.

"You love your Grandpa, eh?" he asked us. He smiled, and we smiled back at him and when we said yes we made sure it was emphatic.

"You'll have it fixed then?" Allan asked.

"Yes, yes. Of course."

"They might be needin' it in a hurry," Allan said and turned to us. "Eh, Milton?"

"Yes," Milton said. "The sooner the better. It can't be too soon."

"All right," Mister Vincent said, walking around the old vehicle and making what seemed an estimate of the repairs it needed.

"What you aim to ask for it?" Allan asked.

I thought that that was a very important question indeed and should have been asked long ago.

Mister Vincent lowered his head. "Well," he began. "I dunno really, Allan. I had this 'ere buggy lying around idle, and the fact is I didn't have no dadburn intention o' having it fixed up. I didn't figger on using it again, so I don't see how I can very well charge a handsome price for it."

Milton looked at me. He was feeling better, I supposed. I too was feeling relieved. However, my heart was still beating heavily.

"Look here," Mister Vincent said, and he led Allan off a little way. They argued and nodded together and smiled and shook hands, like people drawing up a pact. Then Mister Vincent patted Allan on the back and he said,

"Glad to be of help, Allan. Really am."

We left.

"How much does he want for it, Allan?" Milton asked when we reached the gate.

"You'd be surprised," Allan said.

"How much?"

"Guess."

"Twelve pounds?"

"Divide that by two," Allan said, "and subtract one."

"Five!" Milton exclaimed. "Hallelujah! Five!"

"Well, you heard him," Allan said. "He has no more use for it really, an' the price is only that much 'cause he's got to leave off working on other jobs to have it ready."

"Whoopeee!" Milton rejoiced, sweeping off his cap.

"Timmy, did you hear? We can buy it and still be rich!"

"That's what I was thinking," Allan said. "Only I remember a hitch."

"What's that?" Milton asked, simmering down.

"Well, we have the buggy but the problem's not solved. There's no hoss."

"You mean you haven't heard of any going for sale?" Milton said, and suddenly his voice had lost all happiness.

"No. An' even then we can't buy one for eight pounds. That's donkey money. Not hoss money."

Milton was thinking. I wasn't feeling too triumphant now either. I hadn't thought of this hitch. Perhaps we would have to wait until we had built up horse-money with milk sales before the buggy could be brought home.

"Ever hear the saying," Allan said, "a carriage without a hoss?"

"Yes, I've heard it," Milton said, far away.

"Mebbe we better wait till you add to the eight pounds to buy a hoss. You can afford ten shillings a week after collectin' milk money. Save it, then you can buy you a hoss."

"Are you crazy?" Milton barked. He was like a sputtering fuse.

"Now what did I say wrong?" Allan asked.

"Wait! I can't wait and I *won't*."

"But you've go to, Milt. There's no other way."

"There is," Milton said stubbornly.

"Have it your own way," Allan said, and stopped in the road to roll himself a cigarette.

"I've seen donkey carts," Milton said. "I've seen carts drawn by donkeys. So why not a buggy drawn by a donkey?"

"So?"

"So, how about Pal Joe?"

"You out o' your mind or something?" Allan asked with a serious face.

"I'm not either," Milton said fiercely.

Allan was spreading his hands. "But he's young an' he's green an' he's wild like a deer an' not even broken in an' . . ."

"And I'll do it—I'll do it. I can do it."

"Do what?" Allan wanted to know.

"Break him in of course."

"Come on," Allan said, almost amused by Milton's great ambition.

"Do you think I'm afraid?" Milton asked.

"No. That you're afraid, no. But I was jus' wondering . . ."

"What about?" Milton snapped.

"About your gran'pappy. S'ppose he's afraid o' Pal Joe?"

"Afraid? Did you say afraid? Why, Allan?"

" 'Cause Pal Joe is Mirrie's offspring, that's why. 'Member, it was Mirrie that caused the accident, you know. Your gran'pappy could be afraid o' any donkey that's comin' from Mirrie."

"Bah!" Milton said scornfully. "Grandpa afraid! You know better than that, Allan. Grandpa isn't afraid of anything. I ought to make you take that back. No Cassidy is afraid. Are you, Timmy?" he said to me.

"Me? No. I'm not afraid of anything."

"Okay, okay," Allan said, blowing smoke out of his nostrils.

"Grandpa won't be afraid," Milton said.

"Could be I'm wrong," Allan conceded.

"Moreover, Pal Joe will be between two shafts pulling a buggy. That's a good workload to discourage even the most stalwart donkey. You ought to know that, Allan."

"Yes. Maybe you're right at that."

"Of course I'm right," Milton said.

He spat out his words with so much authority that Allan
Bent was completely won over.

"And after I break in Pal Joe he'll be a saint, you bet,"
Milton said.

"Milton," Allan said, looking at him. "If I know you, you'll
do it."

The days that followed were almost as hectic for Milton
as those which had preceded the fair, when all our efforts
had been directed toward preparation for it. Now it was yet
another preparation but this time for the homecoming of the
buggy and its being put to use by Grandpa. Mister Vincent
had given his word to have it roadworthy in a matter of days
and Milton, not wanting to be behind with the draft animal,
spent his days breaking in Pal Joe.

By now Pal Joe had grown into a splendid animal with the
sleek lines of a race horse, and his coat was clean and free of
plant burrs. Pal Joe was strong. He was fast. He possessed
determination. He could kick. He liked prancing. He lowered
his head between his front legs when he was kicking and
prancing. Pal Joe was just great.

Milton had it worked out how he was going to break in
Pal Joe. As arena for the training program, the fairground was
selected. I went to watch them the first day, and after that I
kept on going.

He led Pal Joe in on a rope and tethered him short on a
pole he planted in the ground. Then he proceeded to comb
down the donkey. He combed the sides first, gradually working up to his back and noting, all the while, the burro's
reaction.

Pal Joe swished his tail and tossed his head and made a
hissing sound. But he stamped around excitedly whenever

Milton touched him in the back unexpectedly. That back was the sensitive area, and Milton worked away at it.

"Easy now, Pal Joe," he said as he moved his hand nearer the back. "Easy now, boy." When his hand touched the donkey's back he shivered all over and, continuing, Milton pressed the weight of his hand along the spine. To this Pal Joe reacted by hollowing his back as if he wished to lie down and so get rid of the hand, but Milton continued with the program. Then Pal Joe could stand it no longer and rose on his hind legs and ran around on them much as a ballet dancer, but the shortness of the headrope tethering him restricted his circle.

"Easy, boy," Milton whispered, until the donkey settled down again even to the point of attempting to bite into a bunch of grass. But Milton did not relax the program one bit.

He was at it again, starting with the head and ears, working his hand along the neck to the shoulders and from there to the sides, finally arriving at the back and along that. He did it so often that Pal Joe realized that he wasn't going to be hurt at all and stopped reacting to the hand. So on the second day Milton took the training program a step further.

I carried the equipment that Milton planned to use, a roll of canvas and a bit of rope. He tethered the donkey, shook out the canvas and folded it until it shrunk to a size about a yard square. Carefully now, and while talking to Pal Joe, Milton attempted to set the canvas down on the donkey's back. He was coaxing in his entreaties to Pal Joe.

"Pal Joe, my boy," he said. "Easy now, fellow. Easy now, boy."

But Pal Joe knew that something new was about to happen and was apprehensive. His ears shot up erect and his entire body bristled. Though it wasn't I who was doing the handling, my heart beat fast.

Milton lifted the canvas as high as he could, not wanting it to touch Pal Joe's back at all until it slapped down solidly. He was forced, however, to call up some reserve patience, because each time he lowered the canvas, Pal Joe stamped away. But after a series of attempts, Milton got it down, and the frightened Pal Joe stamped and kicked to unseat the canvas. The canvas didn't budge, however, because Milton, being smart, had wet it and so it clung to Pal Joe despite his resentment.

Voop! he kicked. Vap! Voop!

I guessed he would behave in like manner when Milton took the training to the point of lowering himself onto his back. I wouldn't want to be on his back at all. That burro was wild.

After kicking had failed to rid him of the canvas, Pal Joe stood on his hind legs and did some remarkable ballet dancing, hissing and tugging on his headrope until, finally, he succeeded in unseating the canvas. It had been Milton's aim to tie it down with the bit of rope I had brought along, but with Pal Joe behaving so wild, he didn't have the ghost of a chance.

The following afternoon, though, he did it. He not only got the canvas onto the donkey's back, but he managed to tie it down. Pal Joe reared up and hissed a bit and ballet-danced too, but he soon settled down. The rope which tied the canvas down seemed the strange thing to him and he tried to get at it with his teeth, by bending back his head, but the girth was taut and there wasn't much that Pal Joe could do. He resigned himself. He settled down. A large part of the battle had been won. For Milton, victory was in sight.

"I'll ride him tomorrow," Milton announced when we were headed home.

"Aren't you afraid?" I asked.

"No," he said, truthfully. "But I'll be cautious."

"Wow!" I said. "That will be something—to see you ride him."

"It will be tricky business," Milt admitted.

"Dangerous, the way I saw him prance when you first put the canvas on him," I said.

"Oh, I'll manage. He's getting used to the whole thing."

So the day for the test ride came.

Milton got the canvas onto Pal Joe's back and, after protesting somewhat, the donkey settled down. Then into his mouth went Milt's homemade bit—a slim but strong stick with a rope at each end, these to be the reins.

Some boys had gathered: Onis, Cal Symes, Josh Tingling, Roger Blane. Even Jester. Allan Bent was there too. He was the only invited spectator; the others had invited themselves. Allan had a job to perform. He was to act as a kind of crane to hoist Milton on to Pal Joe's back, as only a direct landing would do.

"All set?" Allan asked.

"Ready," Milton said.

"You're certain you want to get on this ball o' fire, Milt?"

"Why not?" Milt said. "How else am I going to do it?"

"All right," Allan Bent said. "You hold onto those reins plenty tight, 'cause they're what's going to keep you up for a minute or two."

For a minute or two! I thought.

"Yes," Milt said in a tight voice.

"An' keep your legs sucked onto his sides like . . . understand?"

"I understand," Milt said.

"Keep up near his shoulders. Never let him get you out near his loins or back legs. That's where he kicks from an' he will toss you if you get out there."

"Yes," said my brother Milt.

"He'll toss you straight over his head if you get out near 'em back legs."

"I'll keep near his shoulders," Milt said impatiently.

"Good. Ready?" Allan asked.

"Yes," Milt said.

My heart was beating like a tom-tom. The other boys were worked up badly too. Onis, he was goggle-eyed.

Pal Joe's headrope was tied very short to keep him within limits. The moment Allan hoisted Milt up, the donkey's ears shot up erect and he began to paw the ground menacingly. He knew what was about to take place all right, but, for Milt, it was now or never. Allan lowered Milt to the donkey's back.

Pal Joe was like a hurricane, he was so mad. But Milt had the reins securely in his hands, gripping them so tight that he had Pal Joe's neck almost in a bow curve. The donkey's head was just under his curving neck. The prancing continued, a real miniature rodeo right there on Boswell's fairground.

Pal Joe was rearing to go wild, to jump and kick and ballet dance; but Milt was holding his head tightly. He was moving around, however, trying almighty hard to straighten his neck out. But Milt held it curved and Pal Joe shied around on all fours, not jumping, not kicking, not ballet-dancing, just doing some honest-to-goodness shying and prancing.

"You're okay?" Allan Bent asked.

"Yes." Milt's voice was hoarse. He sounded tired.

"Let the headrope out?"

"A little," Milt said.

So Allan did that. He lengthened the tether rope a trifle, giving Pal Joe a bigger circle to describe in his antics. The donkey began to run around now, and Milt continued to hold him.

Jester's mouth was hanging open. The eyes of the other boys were popping out their sockets. Even Allan was as if riding. He was shifting his body, doing the things that Milt did.

"Ride him, Milt," I said. "Ride him!"

Milt continued to hold Pal Joe and his legs were sucking to the donkey's sides, which were now wet. But it seemed Milton's arms were hurting and the reins were burning into his hands, for I noticed that Pal Joe was getting more reins away from him. The donkey was straightening his neck out.

"Hey!" Jester exulted. Milton saw him. He knew now, more than before, that he would have to make this ride a success. Hadn't he mauled Jester in a fist fight? So the bully would be only too pleased now to see the donkey get the better of him.

In my excitement, I began right there to offer a prayer for Milton. But I could not take any part of me away from the ride long enough to finish the prayer.

More reins lost, and Pal Joe's neck straightened out one degree more. That ass seemed as strong as a dinosaur. He captured more reins now and straightened his neck out completely and, when he had this accomplished . . . hallelujah!

Down between his front legs went his head and he became possessed, it seemed, of the devil himself. He kicked as if he meant not only to destroy Milton but also himself, and every time he let loose he made a hissing heeee-heeee sound.

"Ride him, Milt," I encouraged. "Ride him! Break him down!"

But disaster set in. Pal Joe dislodged the bit from his mouth so that the reins in Milt's hands were no longer of any use. Sensibly, Milt discarded them and held onto the burro's mane, which wasn't very long but enough for a desperate rider.

Pal Joe kicked and pranced, but with all his antics he could not unseat Milt. He went on his hind legs and he ran around like that for God knew how long, but Milt was still on his back, grabbing onto that mane. Then he began a wild gallop, zigzagging here and there and Milt, foreseeing each zig and each zag, shifted his body in time and kept his seat. He was hunched forward. He was concentrating. He was like an Apache Brave riding a barebacked stallion.

The boys laughed to see Milt perform.

"Ride him!" Onis chortled happily.

Ride him, yes, but for how long?

Suddenly Pal Joe changed his tactics back to reaching his head between his front legs and Milt, caught off guard, was tossed forward.

"Wow!" Jester exclaimed happily, running around as if he

had just got news that he was winner of a sweepstake. "Wowie!"

The cad!

But Milton was unhurt. He landed on all fours, like a cat, and hurried out of Pal Joe's way. And having achieved his aim, Pal Joe halted his prancing and stopped the whole show. Stopped prancing, everything. Stopped, came to a halt, breathing as if he were going to drop dead with fatigue.

So that was that. The contest was over, and so was the training program. One donkey broken in. Ready for work between the shafts. A defeated donkey. Pal Joe by name.

Everybody walked over to where Milt was.

"That was a good piece o' riding you put on there," Allan said.

"Thanks," Milt said and blew a breath of air out.

"First time a boy ever broke in an animal here in Boswell," Allan went on.

"True?" Milt said, knowing it to be a fact.

"You were great," I told Milt. "If the bit hadn't gotten out of his mouth, you'd still be riding, boy."

"My arms and hands were killing me," Milt said.

Jester didn't want to be left out of it. "First time you ride him, Milton?"

"Yes," Milton told him.

"Boy!" was all Jester said.

After that Milton rode Pal Joe as if he were fooling with a toy. He was the undisputed master of that donkey. Now the buggy could be brought home, and in bypassing a horse we had saved ourselves eight pounds!

··{10}··
The Cloud Comes Home

Mister Vincent was still in possession of the reins he had once used on the horse that pulled the buggy, so we bought them from him and also some other necessary bits of harness. The buggy was finished and we were ready to bring it home and so the three of us—Allan, Milton, and I—went on down to Johnson Corner for it.

To prove that Pal Joe was now a docile and co-operative animal, Milton rode him down. Allan was riding his donkey, too, so I was the only one who walked. Not that I minded it.

The buggy was all ready.

It was cleaned up real smart and sported a new wheel, though it was hard to distinguish the new one from the old, since the carriage was now gleaming in a coat of new paint. It was painted a shiny black and the edges and seams were picked out in white. The canvas top had been patched in places, too, and the hubs were greased. The carriage looked a beauty;

but it was the name it had been given that seemed best of all: *The Cloud!* In large letters and as neat as printing. Standing out in white on the black glossy background. Milton had decided to name it so in honor of Margaret, who had given our stall the name. Since the stall as *The Cloud* had been so great a success, Milton hoped that the buggy as *The Cloud* would follow the stall, not as a money-maker but as a happiness-maker for Grandpa. That was what he said.

Mister Vincent taught Milton the rudiments of harnessing an animal to a buggy.

"See here," he said. "I'll do it slowly again. You watch me now."

His hands moved slowly and his fingers were knowing as he got the leather straps on to Pal Joe, who shied at first but got used to them quickly. He fastened each buckle, got the bit between Pal Joe's teeth, and had the bridle on. And the donkey was all hitched up.

"Now you do it," he said, and Milton took everything off, then put the harness on again, making one mistake only.

"Want to do it again?" Mister Vincent asked.

"Would be glad to," Milton said with more confidence.

" 'Cause practice makes perfect," Mister Vincent said.

So Milton did it again, and he made no mistake the second time. He even improved on the time he took.

"Good," Mister Vincent said. "Good boy. You'll do, you'll do. You'll make a good horseman one day."

"He's got a quick head," Allan Bent said.

"If you ask me," Mister Vincent said, "you don't find boys like these so easily any more."

"You're telling me," Allan Bent said. "They's exceptional boys."

Milton wasn't listening. He was rearing to go. I, too, wished they would stop the chatter. And why not?

Already I was perched upon the seat beside him. Allan paid Mister Vincent and I waved to the old man for Milton and me. Milton shook the reins up and said, "Git"—only that, and Pal Joe strained forward.

The buggy started ahead without a creak. It rolled smoothly and with plenty of spring and bounce in it. Pal Joe handled well for the first time, too.

I looked back through the open rear window and saw Mister Vincent standing in front of his workshop and he was shaking his head. Whether this was from sadness at parting with the buggy or that he was plumb beaten by our spunk, I couldn't have said.

"Get up, Pal Joe," Milton said, shaking the reins. The lively little burro broke into a trot along the gravel road. The wheels crunched the gravel and the metal parts of the harness jingled, and I was so happy. I looked at Allan Bent who rode alongside us on his donkey. I lolled my tongue at him and he squinted back.

Milton let me hold the reins for a while, but I spoiled the whole thing soon. Carried away by excitement, I dropped my foot onto the knob that sounded the gong.

Bing-bong!

The new sound frightened Pal Joe into a gallop. Milton reached across and grabbed the reins quickly away from me and, putting all his strength into the effort, got Pal Joe back under control.

"What did you do that for?" he asked almost breathless. "Stupid!"

"I'm not stupid either."

"You are," he said.

"And what if I hadn't done it?" I argued.

"Pal Joe wouldn't have been frightened into a gallop," he said. "What else?"

"And how would you have discovered, my man, that Pal Joe didn't like the sound?"

"Well . . ." He looked at me and he was gawky.

I would ram my point home. "And supposing I hadn't found that out and Grandpa had touched the gong first time up in the driving seat and Pal Joe bolted off with him? What then?"

"You have a point," he said grudingly.

"Of course! It's a great point too."

All right, all right. No need to rub it in. You win, you win. Through the mischief of Timmy Cassidy, Milton Cassidy has made an important discovery. Rah-rah-rah!"

"You stop rubbing it in now," I told him.

"We'll have to get Pal Joe accustomed to that sound," he said, "but not now."

Having won the argument, I squinted at Allan and he smiled back and wagged his head.

We heard a car coming along the road and Milton wisely pulled the buggy to the side and stopped it. The car soon came into view, roaring at us in top speed and passed, leaving us in a cloud of dust.

"You know something?" Milton said to Allan when we had got going once more.

"No, what?"

"D'you think we're going straight home?"

"No," Allan said. " 'Course not!"

"How not?" Milton asked, as Allan seemed to have read his mind. "If not straight home, where then?"

"Oh," said Allan smiling. "I know all right."

"Where?"

"To the Great House, eh?"

"How did you know?" Milt was taken aback. "You read my mind?"

"No, dear boy. Your heart. I read your heart."

I joined Allan in laughing and Milton blushed, but he got over it by turning his attention to Pal Joe.

"Get up, boy," he said. "Get up and go!" he intoned.

To lighten Pal Joe's load up the hill to the Great House, I jumped down off the buggy; but even so, when he stopped in the yard, Pal Joe was wet with lather and breathing so hard his body seemed to be moving forward and backward, though his legs were stationary. Nobody, it seemed, had seen us arrive, and, wishing to announce his arrival with fanfare, Milton made the mistake I had earlier committed. He slammed his foot down on that gong, not once but thrice, and Pal Joe woke up from his weariness like a devil provoked. But Milton was quick in suppressing this attempt to panic. His hands flicked back with the reins and he was holding them so taut that all the burro managed were unsuccessful attempts at rearing.

Both the gong and the jingling harness had done their job, however—a curtain was drawn from a window and Margaret's face appeared. I saw her face light up and then disappear from the window, and soon she was in the yard with us.

"What a beauty!" Margaret said.

"See what it's been named?"

Margaret blushed.

"I thought you'd like that name," Milt said.

"That's very nice of you," Margaret said, and ran off. When she reappeared from the tremendous bowels of the Great House, she brought her mother along with her.

"Well, well," Mrs. Chaney said as she came up. "At last, at last. It looks so good. Better than I thought. I never suspected it would be this good." She was really smiling.

"And it handles good, ma'am," Milt said.

"Let me try it," Margaret said.

"Sure," Milt said with consummate grace. "Here."

She had already hopped up and she took her seat beside Milton, who passed her the reins. She walked Pal Joe around the big yard to the admiration of us all including Freddy and the two maids, who had popped out to see. Even Mister Chaney looked on from the veranda, but he did not join us in the yard. People used to say that Mister Chaney spent such a lot of time counting his money that he took very little interest in things.

Margaret giggled a lot but she looked good holding the reins and pulling this one to make Pal Joe swing left, and that one to make him turn to the right. But maybe the proudest person of all was Milton. He beamed like the sun.

"When will Mister Cassidy be using it?" Mrs. Chaney asked as Margaret pulled the buggy to a stop beside her.

"Sunday, ma'am," Milton told her.

"New Year's Sunday," commented Mrs. Chaney. "A wonderful present for his New Year, eh? Let's give these two boys a big hand," she said, appealing to the small audience.

And she and Allan and Margaret and Freddy and the two maids clapped so much I had to hide my face for blushes. Margaret was ready to hop down, and playing the gentleman, Milton jumped down first and graciously took her by the hand.

You should have seen them.

As we drove down the hill back to the main road, we passed workers gathering at the estate's office for their pay envelopes. When they saw us in that buggy they were goggle-eyed, so much so that I doubt if they would have improved on their stupefaction had they been looking at a flying saucer manned by Martians.

We didn't have a driveway for *The Cloud* but Allan Bent had, so we drove the buggy into his yard and parked it beneath a tree. Later, when we widened our gate and dug a driveway, we would built a lean-to garage in our yard for *The Cloud*.

When he saw the buggy, Grandpa was even more astonished than the workers we had passed at the plantation office. He had known we had something up our sleeves, but the exact nature of our plans had been kept a secret from him. Neither Milton nor I had let on about the buggy, and Allan Bent and Mrs. Chaney and Margaret had also sworn to keep their mouths shut. They had talked to people about what we were aiming at, in a general sort of way, saying it was to help get Grandpa back to church, but they had never been specific about it. So Grandpa was staggered at the sight of *The Cloud*. He hopped around the buggy unbelievingly and he wanted to know a lot of things in a hurry.

Whose buggy?

Was it a joke that it was his?

How his? How come it was his?

Money we made from the fair had bought it? Impossible! Nonsense! Who from? Mister Vincent at Johnson Corner? Rubbish! Dratted nonsense! "Allan, you ever hear such a cock-an'-bull story?"

But Allan wasn't talking yet.

What made us decide on a buggy?

For him to go to church in? Really? Jehovah! And we had hidden it from him all this while! We had never let on! Allan was in on it, too—the hiding of the scheme from him. Pranksters! We were all pranksters and Mrs. Chaney and her daughter too. He'd be doggoned!

"I never could have guessed what was goin' on," he said

to Allan. "I never knew they could have done it."

"Mista Cassidy," Allan said, "the children of today's plenty clever."

"Eh?" Grandpa said. "They's mighty clever, eh, Allan? In our days we couldn't have done it. We wouldn' have thunk o' it even. But then, David killed Goliath, eh, Allan? The li'l shepherd boy gone an' killed an armed giant. But I never knew they could have done it."

Grandpa hugged us and he kissed us and he sang our praises and, together with Allan and Mrs. Bent, he went on saying good things about us two for probably as long as an hour.

The word soon got around that we had brought home a buggy called *The Cloud*, as shiny as the stars of the night sky. Allan Bent's yard began to fill up and soon it looked like an exhibition site, so many villagers came to see the buggy. The boys were there—Cal and Onis and Josh and Roger and all the rest of them. Why, their expressions seemed to be saying, why hadn't we thought of something as worthwhile as this? But then, how could they have done anything like it? We had a grandpappy who had lost his leg in an accident and also his attendance at church; what had they? Nothing. Therein lay the difference, the big difference. Therein lay our incentive. We had a goal and we had worked at it and now we were there, thank God.

This, of course, was Friday and, steamed up as we were, we could hardly await the arrival of Sunday, the almighty big day when Grandpa would return to church for the first time since the accident. Return, moreover, in style.

He was looking forward to it no less than we were, and spent the better part of Saturday sunning one of his Sunday suits. Later he called in the village barber. This man traveled with his equipment in a small box and, to perform a haircut, he needed only to have a bench for his client to sit on and a tree to provide shade. So Grandpa got his haircut right on our veranda. On Saturday night he commandeered me to polish his boot "until you can see your face in it, son," which was what I did. Sunday morning found him indulging in an early toilet. Standing in front of the hand mirror which he hung on a peg in a veranda post, he used his razor with meticulous care and whipped his unruly beard and mustache into shape. He was even humming to himself, which was a sure sign of his contentment.

So the big day came, and what a day! Milton and I ran off to Sunday school with an assurance from Allan Bent that he would harness Pal Joe for Grandpa.

To be frank, I learned nothing at all in Sunday School. I was aware that, like Milton, I had become a hero in Boswell, one of a couple; and all I wished to see happen was for *The Cloud* to come up the hill to the church, with Grandpa shaking up the reins.

Sunday school was over and not too soon, for I had begun to pop with excitement at having to sit quietly in one place. The church was filling up.

Easter Sunday, Christmas Sunday, and New Year Sunday were three days on which all churches were guaranteed to be full. All those people who had not bothered themselves on the other Sundays in the year to go to church, turned out on these three days, dressed in clothes that had not seen the sun for entire seasons. Women in frothy frills and skirts starched stiff, lace-trimmed bodices and organdy skirts. Men dressed in old and new fashions, some looking like bears just out of a long period of hibernation. People singing in off-key voices because it had been such a long time ago since they last made a joyful noise unto the Lord.

Inside the church was hot and I was glad to go outside into the cool air that blew across the ridge on which the church stood.

A car tooted and we heard the engine and, as was customary among the boys, we crowded into the front yard to see the car arrive. Parson Jackson's maybe. But no. Not his. This was big. It was black. I knew it too. The Chaneys' car. It came slowly up the hill in low gear, Mister Chaney at the wheel.

Mister Chaney was another of the three-Sunday church-goers and here he was now, with Mrs. Chaney beside him in the front seat and Margaret in the back, sitting on the edge of the seat the better to see ahead. Margaret came straight up to Milton and me. She smiled. She was very beautiful. She was in pure white, and around her neck there was a necklace of gold with a small cross as its pendant.

"Hello," she said in the nicest voice. I wouldn't mind being where she was at all times if for only one thing: the way she enunciated. I nodded at her and, in agitation now, continued to watch the road.

"We just passed him down the road," she said to Milton.

"Who?" I asked. "Grandpa?"

"Yes," she said, and nodded too.

As I continued to watch the road I saw them. First Pal Joe, then Grandpa, then the bulk of the buggy behind him. Pal Joe labored slowly up the hill and almost the whole church was looking on because the secret had leaked out.

Suddenly and from nowhere, Allan Bent joined us. He was another irregular churchman, but he had to be there, I guessed, to see Grandpa make his comeback, this triumphal entry. Allan's jacket was too short for him and his trousers could have done with a little pressing and there were other things not perfect about his dress, but I wasn't in a mood to find more faults. Not with Grandpa coming up the hill into the church-yard now.

Grandpa pulled up under a large tamarind tree, and he hitched his reins with aplomb, and all the old men who were gathered outside began to walk down to him. But Milton and I beat them to the buggy and we helped Grandpa down from it.

He swung out on his crutches, but soon was intercepted by the host of well-wishers, and he must have squeezed nearly fifty hands in greeting. We joined Margaret at the church steps. She was smiling and was no less proud than we were, and why shouldn't she be?

Parson Jackson's Morris car now chugged to a stop in the yard and everybody started to enter the church. Inside suddenly became quieter than inside a library and the piety was so pronounced you could almost feel it. Only the bell outside made any sound.

I turned and looked through the open window to the tree from which the bell was hanging and saw Grandpa standing nearby, he and Parson Jackson, and Manuel Copeland, who was some sort of deacon. Grandpa, it seemed, was recalling the past, because he said something and Jabesh Gilligan stepped aside, giving way to him. My Grandpappy got hold of that bell clapper and gave the bell a few merry bashes, and everybody in the little knot outside laughed. I had known he would want to ring that bell again, if only to recall old times. He didn't ring it long: he merely wished to handle it once more to celebrate his return to church.

Now they came toward the church and entered by way of the vestry. I wished the rector would start the service, because my neck was hurting from twisting round to look back down the aisle at what was going on there.

Everything was quiet until Grandpa left the vestry for his seat near the rear of the congregation. He managed to muffle the stamping sound of his crutches on the floorboards, but not so his one boot. What I mean is, he had no intention of silencing the boot he wore on his good foot. He wasn't the one to wear boots that weren't proficient in the business of squeaking, and this single boot squeaked well and everybody looked around at him. Believe me, he went on to make a mighty show of taking his seat.

He stood there and slowly leaned up his crutches against the wall, slowly, very slowly indeed; and then he took out his handkerchief and spread it out on the pew where he was about to sit. Then he sat down and leaned forward to pray.

Parson Jackson got himself up into the pulpit to give out the text. It was the longest sermon I ever heard him deliver. He had always been in a hurry to have done at our church to go to some other mission station, but on this New Year's Sunday, he took his time. He welcomed all the three-Sunday churchgoers, but a special welcome was extended to Grandpa after his terrible accident. Somebody must have tipped off the rector about Grandpa's buggy and the effort behind it, for next he went deep into the subject of self-help. Then he became personal and told our story, Milton's, Margaret's, and mine. He even mentioned *The Cloud*, the stall, and *The Cloud*, the buggy, and he ended by saying that this was indeed the cloud with the silver lining.

Everybody's eyes, it seemed, were fastened on us. I had never before heard so many groans from a congregation in one church service, and the quality of a church service in Boswell was judged by the number of groans it forced out.

There was a hymn following the sermon, and I clearly picked out Grandpa's bass as he roared from the rear like the lion of Judah. It was during this hymn-singing too, that the collection was taken. You should have seen Jabesh Gilligan. He was in the aisle with the collection plate and his chest was thrust out like a pigeon in the act of courting. When I looked back at Grandpa, he didn't seem to mind very much that Jabesh was doing his old job now. He was happy merely to be there.

Then it was communion time, and when it came Grandpa's turn, he squeaked his way up the aisle with the aid of Jabesh Gilligan, and he knelt erect and magnificent at the altar. My Grandpappy.

After that, Grandpa went regularly to church, and not only that: he resumed, on a larger scale than before, his basket craft. The coming of the buggy had indeed wrought a miracle, injecting new life into him, and once again my Grandpappy was a man on the go. It was pretty to see him on a Saturday morning setting out to market, baskets and fishpots filling the buggy and hanging from its sides as well.

Now that I am grown up and can look back at that time in our lives, I think how much it did for us, especially for Milton. After that he was well on his way to manhood. In fact, he became a man long before he was twenty-one. By the time he was sixteen he had developed a man's awareness of responsibility, especially for Grandpa, who was growing older and weaker.

In time he left school and went to work for Mister Chaney on his plantation, starting as a bookkeeper. He earned enough to hire a maid to give Grandpa the woman's care he now needed, and me he bundled off to a secondary school. But although, as a result, I have had more formal education than he, I haven't done nearly as well as he has. Because he is now virtual owner of the vast Chaney estate, or rather, co-owner. He courted and married Margaret, the only daughter and heiress.

Grandpa has died; yes, he has. The old lion finally went down with pneumonia in the wet month of May, 1959, and Milton and I laid him out to rest beneath the guango tree in the yard in which he had spent most of his days. Mister Chaney also is dead. He went from a heart-attack, and Mrs. Chaney lives with Milton and Margaret in the Great House.

Things are different on the Chaney estate now. Milton put into effect new ideas on the running of it, and the result is a first-class farm on scientific lines. Bananas are still grown, and so is sugar cane, but their acreage has been drastically reduced so that space is provided for dairy-cattle—Milton's first love— chickens, and a coconut grove, complete with small copra and coir factories.

Milton's fields are fertilized with farmyard manure from his pasture, and a truck picks up his milk to the railway station at Montpelier, from whence it is shipped to the Bog Walk Condensary. His chickens and his eggs find their way onto the plates of the swank north-coast hotels, and his copra goes to make margarine and cooking oil. Coir from his small but efficient factory makes mattresses. Whenever I glimpse this factory I remember our grass-filled mattresses of yesteryears, but change! change!

Sure, Milton has done well.

He has children now too, a boy—Milton Bradley—and a girl—Ann Margaret. Wonderful children.

I am yet unmarried and my Christmases are spent, every one of them, at the Chaney Great House.

The sugar cane still shoot arrows against the sky and the wind of Christmas still comes up the valley, carrying the special scents of the season on its breath, but there is much that has been lost since we knew Christmas spent with Grand-pa. The firecrackers are fewer on Christmas Eve, the John Canoe dancers do not appear any more, and the music of the homely orchestra has been replaced by blaring canned stuff.

But there are some things we still have. Margaret still bakes at Christmas, and there is the fair too. Milton and I boyishly set off a few firecrackers in the yard on Christmas morning, and there is a punch, though the stout we now use to make it has been demilitarized and doesn't behave in the same way as the frothing, seething porter of the good old days. Though Milton can afford turkey for dinner—and there always is—we also have curried goat, which is a must.

There is always a kind of happy expectancy at the dinner table until someone says: "Well?"

And someone else suggests, "Let's go look at it." Or something like that.

This is followed by happy laughter and we go out, all of us, Mrs. Chaney and the children too, to look at the museum piece which Milton has had removed to his large garage—now disused but forever symbolic, *The Cloud.*

About the Author

C. EVERARD PALMER *was born and brought up in Kendal, Jamaica, a village just like Boswell in this story. Indeed he himself says that it was "peopled by citizens with a remarkable taste for gaiety, especially at Christmas. The flavor is essentially that of the district."*

Mr. Palmer, a teacher, has had articles published in Jamaica's leading newspaper, and has written two successful adventure stories for the Jamaican Ministry of Education. This is his first book to be published in America.